THE ELYSIUM PROPOSAL

by A.E. Bross

Where We Converge
Copyright © 2023 by A.E. Bross
Cover Design © The Cover Collection

First Edition, 2023
Paperback ISBN: 979-8-9877561-3-3
EPUB ISBN: 979-8-9877561-2-6
Amazon ASIN: B0CHQVPZ2J

CONTENT NOTE

This book contains brief mention of xenophobia and complicated, sometimes toxic family dynamics and behavior. Please be kind to yourself while reading.

For everyone who has ever wanted that one night to go smoothly.

I.

Kyle's gut was a tangle of nerves that squirmed unpleasantly as she fixed her short, dark hair in the looking glass. With a huff, she pulled at her sleeves, hoping that straightening them would put the finishing touches on an outfit that made her look more the dashing ship's captain and less the anxious suitor. Yes, she *was* both; she just didn't want to *look* both.

She adjusted her clothing in the mirror of her cabin, fiddling with the edges of the collar that showed beneath her fine blue coat, the one of elegant brocade. She wore new, spotless black trousers and a clean white shirt, the material pristine, the top few buttons left open to make it low and revealing. Her father had given her the captain's coat just that past solstice. She only ever took it out on special occasions, and it looked spectacular if she did say so herself.

And she did.

Not that that would matter. Regardless of how poorly or well planned, what came next wasn't up to her. When not even her signature swagger and confidence could assuage her fears, she let her shoulders drop in defeat. "I don't know if I can do this," she muttered. The ring box in her coat pocket was making her ensemble and her mood heavier, weighing it all down with expectations and anxiety.

"Did you say something, Captain?" asked Markham. Gilbert Markham, a wiry slip of a man, was *The Stargazer*'s First Mate and Kyle's most trusted friend. He sat at a small desk, Kyle's desk, in the captain's quarters, his long legs somehow folded comfortably beneath it as he scribbled notes on a piece of parchment. Organized and detail-

1

oriented, skills Kyle was sorely lacking, he was likely balancing the books before taking the silver they'd need to pay for docking fees at the Saltskiff Bazaar's port office. The fees weren't cheap, and *The Stargazer* wasn't known to travel with an overabundance of funding. Careful bookkeeping was a must and much beyond Kyle's abilities.

Markham was often the only thing that kept them afloat, financially speaking.

"She said what I am sure she has been saying for days now," came another voice, low and teasing, from the doorway. "Just venting these endless anxieties about one task or another."

At the entrance of the captain's quarters, her quarters, her older half-brother Nico grinned at her. In her worried preparations, Kyle hadn't heard the door open, much less someone enter. She was immediately hit with the annoying mixture of dismay and relief only a sibling could bring. A familiar face was always welcome, but his jesting was not. He was leaning against the doorjamb, arms crossed over his chest, a smug look on his irritatingly handsome face.

Kyle and Nico had both inherited their father's dark hair and brown eyes. Some claimed they also shared a glint in their smiles, a genetic predisposition to a cat-that-got-the-canary sort of grin. That was where the similarities ended. Where Nico had been blessed with a jawline that could make anyone of any inclination swoon, Kyle's features were softer, her heart-shaped face more rounded. Kyle was also much shorter than Nico, her head only reaching beneath his shoulders, and where Nico had rich, tawny brown skin that deepened to a warm russet beneath the high sun of Sursum, Kyle had inherited her mother's pale, sensitive skin. As a result of a life on the open waters, she was completely covered with freckles.

"Shut your gob, Nico," Kyle snapped, though she softened her words with a nearly concealed smile. She didn't have a bad relationship with him, but he liked to tease, and her nerves were in no state to handle any of his ribbing. "I don't recall inviting you onto my ship."

He rolled his eyes, pushing off of the doorjamb and strolling into her quarters. "*You always have an open invitation aboard* The Stargazer," he said, his tone high in an exaggerated mimicry of Kyle's voice.

Clearly, he needed to have a doctor check his hearing; Kyle knew her warm alto sounded nothing like that.

Chuckling, Nico let his voice drop to its normal baritone as he took up the cushioned window seat on the opposite side of the cabin, staring out the glass and to the sea beyond. "I believe that was, what? Last summer solstice? Or was it the one before?" He glanced at her, grinning in a boyish delight only displayed when he was trying to get under his younger sister's skin.

"I was under the influence of far too much port wine when I spoke those words," Kyle grumbled. She was unable to deny his claim; she had a rough recollection of it, despite the many servings—or perhaps it had been bottles—of spirits she had imbibed that particular solstice. "And it was the summer before last. Besides, as captain, I could rescind that offer."

"You *could*, but you won't."

"Won't I?"

He shifted on the seat, staring expectantly. Daring her.

She narrowed her eyes at him, hating that he was absolutely right. Very few could maintain anger at Nico Talos for long, and she was no exception. She relented, her annoyance melting to further fuel her nearly forgotten anxiety. "Fine, but just please don't make things worse."

"Captain?" asked Markham after politely clearing his throat.

Kyle had forgotten the first mate was still there. "Yes?"

"Permission to pay the docking fees and be off?"

Kyle nodded. "Go on. Tell Bonnie I said hello and mess with the kiddo's hair for me, will you?"

Nico followed Markham to the door and, once the first mate was gone, closed the door to the cabin, leaning against it as he turned back to Kyle. "How long did you give the crew for shore leave?" he asked.

"The week," Kyle replied with a shrug. "We all need a break."

Nico's expression softened. "What do you have planned?" he asked after a pause. He'd taken the time to measure his half-sister's demeanor, and from the uneasiness in his voice, he had decided to try and help.

Oh no. This was *worse* than the teasing.

3

For a brief moment, Kyle considered not telling him. It would serve him right for acting like such a pompous ass. Besides, while he meant well, Nico had a history of being less-than-successful when it came to any sort of relationship. Being a servant to the Sursum Navy and a soft touch as well, he never quite mastered his father's rakish skills. It was probably for the best, but it also made Nico ill-equipped to help in matters of love.

"A romantic evening," Kyle admitted.

"And that entails?"

"Bess promised to cook us their favorite meal. It will be brought to their room so that we don't have to interrupt our evening by dining in the tavern proper." As she explained her plans, she paced the width of the cabin. While *The Stargazer* was a grand ship, her size didn't truly compare to her larger seafaring brethren, which meant the captain's cabin was also relatively diminutive. Not cramped, but Kyle didn't enjoy the lavish day cabin and living quarters that her brother or other captains with larger ships did. Her own captain's quarters provided her ample room to traverse repeatedly when her nerves got the better of her.

Nico grimaced. "You're not even taking them someplace nice? Just staying at their family's inn and tavern?"

Kyle stopped her pacing when she was near the desk, leaning against it and crossing her arms over her chest. This was rich. "Says the man who couldn't remember his partner's birthday."

"I am never living that down, am I?"

"Not when you both shared the same birthday!"

Nico hung his head in shame, as he should.

"Besides, there is no such thing as 'nicer' at Saltskiff. Their family runs one of the best places on the docks. You won't find better, just those on an even keel." Kyle was getting defensive on her partner's behalf, and she didn't care. She stood up just a bit straighter. Here, she knew better. "They're also not going to want to go out on the town after a long day of work, which I know they will have had. It's a family establishment, and they work and live there." Her voice had risen, a not-so-subtle hint for her sibling to drop that avenue of conversation.

Nico raised his hands in surrender, rushing to change the topic. "All right, my apologies. So, after this glorious dinner, what next?"

Kyle felt the heat of a blush warm her cheeks, but she refused to be embarrassed in front of Nico. Instead, she raised an eyebrow and offered him a smirk of her own. She was absolutely thrilled that he had walked into this, and she struggled to keep the joy from her face. "Well, one thing will probably, hopefully, lead to another. There will be kissing, disrobing, and then—"

"Stop!" Nico snapped, his hands flying to cover his ears, eyes wide with horror. He looked boyish and silly, trying to protect himself from hearing what might come next. "Bite your tongue. Don't you dare finish that sentence. I do not want to know that about my little sister."

"But didn't you want all of the details?" she asked, affecting the caricature of an innocent expression.

"*Kyle!*" he nearly shrieked.

"You asked." Kyle cackled with laughter but relented. "Poor Nico, such an easy target."

He hesitated before lowering his hands, eyes narrowed with suspicion. "I come here to see how my little sister is doing, and this is the thanks I get?"

Kyle rolled her eyes. "You came here to see Da and because you get bored on shore leave."

"*And* to see how you were doing," he insisted. "Regardless, Da and I will make sure *The Stargazer* is well taken care of while you and your crew are ashore." He chuckled. "If anyone can call Saltskiff 'ashore.'"

Nico wasn't wrong. What the world knew as the Saltskiff Bazaar had started off as a tiny island, barely large enough to hold a long boat. Because of its location, in the middle of everything and with nothing surrounding it, Saltskiff became an ideal place for the less than reputable ones among the Archipelago to trade spoils and stolen goods. The privateers and pirates of those days had deemed it a neutral ground, and even naval forces from differing countries respected it. The Bazaar expanded, but in a patchwork manner that it was now infamous for. As time went on, ships, rafts, and other vessels, some seaworthy, some less so, attached themselves to those docks. So much so that they formed different neighborhoods. Eventually, trade brought others, businesses lashing their ships and hopes together. Homes were built. The bazaar blossomed, a strange flower made of ships and boats of all sizes, held together by docks for roads and bridges. What had started out as a ragtag group of ruffians and riffraff looking to barter ill-gotten gains had grown into a metropolis on the sea.

"Don't let Da steal my ship," Kyle warned, only half joking.

"I won't," he insisted, hands raised in surrender.

"Don't you steal my ship, either."

"Why would I bother? I have a better one."

Again, he was correct. Captain Nico Talos, lately of his majesty of Sursum's navy, was on leave only until the next war was declared and the need for naval battles began anew. Nico's ship, the *SMS Hesperides*, easily dwarfed *The Stargazer*. His was an eighty-gun frigate that had yet to know defeat in battle. It had come close only once, in an encounter with the pirate Fairbanks, but the pirate had withdrawn first, and the *Hesperides* had won the day.

Nico never let people forget it, either.

Kyle hated that it had such a reputation. It meant it was targeted more often. She was lucky in that Sursum's navy also highly valued the ship, and it had been docked since the last war ended a year before. The idea of war was repugnant to her, and not only because it put Nico in danger. War was horrendous. In her heart of hearts, she hoped there would never be another, though she never told anyone this, lest they think she had gone soft.

As an independent contractor—what most would call a pirate or mercenary ship—Kyle had always been careful to keep herself allegiance-free. She took all of the legal jobs that she came across and some that perhaps toed the line, but she kept to the Archipelago and liked it that way.

A war could ruin that.

Then again, if he had no navy to occupy him, Nico might spend more time aboard *The Stargazer*.

Perish the thought.

"All right, enough delay. The last of the day is fading, and I'm expected at *Port in the Storm*." She checked her coat pocket one final time to make sure the ring box was still there before moving to the door. Nico stepped to the side and opened it for her. As she strode past him, into the hall and towards the deck, she hesitated for a moment, throwing a sideways glance his way. "Stay out of trouble, Nico, and keep my ship safe. That's an order."

Nico shrugged, flashing his boyish smile. "Not a problem for me. Da, on the other hand…" He trailed off, shrugging helplessly as if that would explain everything that needed to be said about their father.

"Then keep Da out of trouble as well." Kyle had to keep from whining and instead rolled her eyes and continued on. Sometimes it was damned frustrating how very similar the Talos father and son could be.

2.

The sound of the damp wood creaking and groaning beneath Kyle's feet was a comfort as she strode the broad dock boards, weaving between local denizens and first-time visitors to the Bazaar on her way to her destination. This was the Silvermoon district, so named for its comfortable and affordable accommodations. One needed only a handful of silver to purchase a soft bed and meal that wouldn't upset the stomach. Silvermoon was as much a haven for the respected merchant as it was for the ruffian pirate with delusions of standing in the community. It was also far busier than usual. That was not a good sign. More people meant more customers and more customers meant more work for the very person she was going to see. Kyle fought to hold onto her confidence and optimism in the face of the thickening crowds.

She *would* make sure she and her love enjoyed themselves. This evening would go well, damn it. No one was going to prevent her from carrying out these plans. Kyle had put too much effort into choosing the best time of year, planning it with a few hand-chosen confidants, and selecting the perfect ring to give up now. Failure was not an option.

Port in the Storm was one of the few structures in the district that had been built more to resemble a building one might find on land rather than an actual boat. Oh, it was built to float, but whereas many other establishments were converted frigates, even a warship or two, the *Port* had been built with the idea of terra firma in mind. It more resembled an inn at a port town than one found in the Saltskiff Bazaar.

And from the front of that cozy-looking inn, there eschewed a line of impatient customers, extending out of the door and along the seawater-slicked dock, all of them barely keeping their tempers in check as they waited for entry. Kyle suspected that the only thing keeping them from violence was the risk of losing their spot in the line. She also recognized more than one face in the progression, and she feared that a few would remember a debt or two that she *might* owe them, should they see her. Intimidating, to say the least. The chances were higher than zero of things turning ugly, but she refused to let that disrupt the night.

Pulling the collar of her coat up to hide her face behind the thick fabric, she hunched her shoulders to look shorter. She cursed herself for not wearing a hat, but this would have to do. Trying to blend with surrounding passersby, she walked quickly past the line of hungry, would-be patrons and slipped into the door as someone else was exiting, successfully hiding herself in plain sight.

The entryway of the *Port in the Storm* was small, crowded into more of a narrow hallway than an actual foyer. After a stride or two in, the wall opened on the right to allow for a built-in desk. Behind it was a tall reed of a woman. Her straw-colored hair was pulled back in what might have been a practical bun at the beginning of the day but had become half-undone. Her no-nonsense features were only partially visible, her head very nearly buried in the pile of papers before her. The heavy scratching of a quill against the coarse surface was somehow audible as the woman wrote, despite the din from within and without the establishment.

Kyle barely had time for a breath of relief. As soon as she cleared the doorframe, the woman behind the desk spoke, her disinterested voice announcing, "No rooms left for the night. If you want a meal, you'll have to be getting back out there and to the back of the line. No cutting and no trouble."

"Bess, it's me," Kyle hissed, letting her collar fall to reveal her face. She straightened a bit as well.

"Who is me?" the woman, Bess, snapped. She finally looked up from the papers before her. Kyle could see she had been drawing and crossing out circles and squares and assumed her work was a desperate attempt at keeping track of what tables in the establishment had been taken and which might soon be free to seat new patrons at.

Bess's impatience melted away, and a smile brightened her lined face. "Oh, Kyle. Sorry. It's been so busy. Fairbanks's entire fleet docked on the north side of the Bazaar, and all flooded into Silvermoon." Bess thought for a moment, stroking under her chin with the feather of the quill. "Speaking of Fairbanks, you may want to avoid being seen by too many sets of eyes. Isn't Lamark one of their people? Don't you still owe him for that—"

"Shhh," Kyle cautioned, glancing around. "Besides, I'd heard he'd been smitten by a merman. Hopefully, that will keep him busy and away from Saltskiff."

Bess sighed, momentarily resting her elbow on the counter, head in hand. "Lamark with a mer? Some people have all the luck." She was wistful for a moment, then shook her head, straightening up. No time for daydreaming, not for Bess. When she refocused her attention on Kyle, she wore a worryingly apologetic expression. "Anyway, we have been swamped."

Kyle could hear the crackling sound of her well-laid plans beginning to split.

If they had been so busy, did that mean that the dinner she had sent word to Bess about was no longer an option? Determined not to allow her schemes to be completely broken, Kyle pushed forward. After all, every challenge was an opportunity to defeat it, yes? "I can see you've been beset." She nodded towards the dining room, just in time to see a wooden flagon, empty thankfully, sail over the heads of the crowd. It was followed by loud demands for more beer. Charming. "How have you been holding up? Is Teague still serving in the dining room?"

Please say no. Please say no.

Bess shook her head. "Ethan and Kasy came in looking for extra coin, so I put them to work. I know you and Teague had this night planned, so I gave Teague the time off and put the other two to work." She grinned knowingly. "You two will have each other all to yourselves."

All right, that's a good sign.

"And, uhm, how were they feeling?" Kyle's voice shook with her nerves.

"Not in the best moods, as you could imagine. They were relieved to be free of this rabble." Bess straightened the papers before her and gave Kyle a sympathetic look. "Don't worry so much. I'll send up a bottle of the good wine and a couple of treats as soon as I can. It's all we can spare right now."

"But the dinner..." Kyle trailed off, more cracks and crumbles rending her plan to smaller and smaller bits.

"What do we have to do to get some service around here?" came a shout from the doorway, followed by a gust of humid, salty air.

Kyle was nearly bowled over as a tall, broad beast of a man stalked in, his face sanguine with impatience. "We've been waitin' nigh—"

"You'll wait a bit longer if you know what's good for you, ya picaroon," Bess bellowed, interrupting him with a volume and authority that shook the very walls.

The big man, who seconds before had been swaggering and confident, wielding his heft with violence in mind, turned a greenish shade of pale and retreated back out the door and into the approaching night. Kyle shook her head.

"As I was saying," Bess began, her look of disgust following the man despite the door now being between them. "I know you had designs for the evening. I didn't expect this either. I'm sorry about your dinner, but you see what I'm dealing with."

More of her plan disintegrated. Kyle barely kept from whining. "It happens," she managed.

Bess leaned forward conspiratorially. "None of this riff-raff will be here come the morning, and those that are will be wanting to sleep it away. How about an extravagant breakfast, instead?" She pointed to the people crowding the entryway and dining room. "Do they look like early risers?" She gave Kyle a sad, guilty expression. "It's the best I can do."

Kyle pursed her lips. If she was being honest, it wasn't enough, but she wasn't going to tell Bess that. She could see Bess was doing her utmost to salvage what she could. It would have to do. If her life on the seas had taught Kyle anything, it was that one had to make the best of a situation. She swallowed a growl of frustration and forced herself to at least attempt some cheer. She straightened up and gave a decided nod. She *could* rescue this occasion from the jaws of defeat. "Very well. Tomorrow morning, then. And don't forget the wine and sweets tonight?"

Bess nodded and gestured for her to head up.

A.E. Bross

Kyle wove her way through the dining room. On a night with a normal crowd, the space had always seemed more than ample. Now, filled to the brim with privateers, sailors, and naval officers who had no wars to distract them, it was a cacophonous mess of moving bodies, sloshing drinks, and raucous laughter. Any other time Kyle would be in her element, carousing with the rest of them. A few patrons even recognized her, cheering or offering a wave as she went past. They shouted slurred, ale-soaked invitations to join them. Kyle remembered Bess's warning about Fairbanks and groaned inwardly, praying to whatever deity might listen that his men were not present in the establishment. While she had no fear for health or safety, she knew having to settle her debts would take more patience and persuasion than she had at her disposal at the moment. Best to avoid the situation altogether. Too many seafaring folks wanted to settle scores with drinking wagers, and while Kyle had the stamina, she lacked the time.

Kyle had a bit of a reputation with the regulars at her favorite haunts. Despite inheriting her mother's lack of stature, she had also received a constitution that could rival someone three times her size when it came to drink. Very few newcomers she met could pick her out as anything but a local, and it wasn't until she had drunk them under the table that she admitted that she was Adalarian on her mother's side. A millennium or two of brewing and imbibing some of the strongest spirits known in all the lands was bound to have an effect on a group of people's tolerance, one that they passed to their children. *Thanks, Ma.*

Kyle gave a gracious nod to the invitations but didn't slow. Moving past the stairs at the back of the dining hall that led to rented guest rooms, she continued through the swinging door beyond them, careful not to knock the rickety wood from its frame. The hinges were old and liable to give up at any moment. Once through, she found herself in the first of two kitchens the tavern had. This was the smaller of them and was kept for food that needed no heat to prepare. It helped to keep the dining room tolerantly cool on warm or busy nights.

Still, the smells of cooking were thicker here, and Kyle's mouth watered at the rich scent of stew and mutton coming from the inner kitchen and the colorful fresh vegetables and fruit that were being

12

prepared around her. She cursed the busyness of the night and Fairbanks's arrival. If it hadn't been for them, she would be enjoying those savory and sweet delights.

Concentrate on the positive. Nothing can be saved by whining.

The small kitchen forced Kyle to sidestep and elude faster. She was barely able to avoid getting in the way of the servers running to and fro collecting food and drink for the patrons of the dining room. She veered to the side and vanished into an alcove. The small space housed cramped stairs that led to the much smaller third floor, where Bess and her two siblings lived. The other members of the Dailann family lived elsewhere in the Bazaar; they simply owned this and two other establishments. The Dailann brood was plentiful, and all expected to help in the inns when they came of age. From what Kyle had been told, all of Silvermoon could be populated by them and their kin.

Kyle strode down the hall and paused at the door at the end. Her destination.

The heft of the ring box in Kyle's pocket doubled with her nerves, and she shifted her weight from foot to foot, butterflies waging war in her belly. She stood a bit straighter, smoothed any wrinkles from her clothes, and knocked on the thick wooden door.

"Yes?" came a muffled voice from the other side.

"I-It's Kyle," she announced, trying to smooth over the waver in her voice.

There was a shuffling sound from within the room, then the door opened, and Kyle let out what felt like all of the breath in her very being in one huge sigh of relief.

Teague Dailann stood silhouetted against the light of their small room, a warm glow cast by two hanging lanterns within. Tall alongside the doorframe, the shadow that their graceful form cast fell cool on Kyle, a relief from the loudness and brightness of the rooms below. Teague's long, flaxen hair, normally kept in a tight plait, flowed over their shoulders in luxurious waves, and Kyle had to wonder if they had put a warm iron to it to give the locks such beautiful shape and bounce. Despite looking tired, Teague's face was alight with joy when they saw Kyle, and

13

they grinned, elegant features practically shining, hazel eyes glittering. "I have been looking forward to seeing you for days," they announced.

Kyle would never cease being amazed at how Teague's very presence had the ability to wash away the world. Her muscles loosened, and her jaw relaxed. Everything felt better. When they were together, anything beyond the two of them fell away.

Before Kyle could form a response, Teague dipped their head, lips seeking out Kyle's own for a deep, enthusiastic kiss that the pirate captain could do little but sink into. Almost without realizing it, she wrapped her arms around Teague's waist, pulling them closer until nothing separated them but the clothes they wore. The smell of soap and the sweet citrus scent of verbena reached Kyle, and she smiled into the kiss. The verbena was a perfume oil she had brought Teague on her last visit to Saltskiff. Kyle silently congratulated herself on choosing a fragrance that suited Teague so well.

Pressing against her love felt so good to Kyle, like being home, and she wanted more. Her yearning fueled her passions as she stepped into the room, Teague retreating a step to allow her in. Kyle kicked the door shut, sliding the bolt home before turning back to Teague. The momentary absence of kissing had suddenly been too much for both of them, and they were together again, arms intertwined, hungry and wanting.

"I missed you so," Kyle breathed between kisses, fingers running through Teague's hair, palms cradling their cheeks.

"As I missed you," Teague cooed as their slender, graceful hands slid up, deftly relieving Kyle of her captain's coat. "We should get reacquainted as soon as possible."

Distantly, Kyle thought of the ring. The missed dinner. The proposal. Her nerves. They were all far off, though, obscured in the mist of desire and love that had swept in.

Without the coat in their way, Teague took hold of the fine material of Kyle's shirt and gave it a tug, freeing it from her waistband. Kyle shuddered as her lover's cool hands touched her skin beneath the fabric. She was lost. There was no cohesive thought that could be formed as she arched towards Teague's caress. Warmth flooded through her, and she rested her hands on Teague's hips, a breathy moan escaping her barely parted lips.

"What was that, Captain? Did you say something?" Teague asked with a playful lilt in their voice. Their hands moved upwards beneath the material of Kyle's fine shirt, fingers brushing the underside of her breasts.

"Gods, Teague, don't tease." Kyle's eyelids fluttered, pleasure making her skin tingle and the junction of her thighs throb. "Please, I just...I missed you... I wanted to..." She couldn't keep a coherent thought in her mind, much less speak one. Now was not the time. She was barely aware when Teague lifted her shirt upwards, the fabric gliding quickly and effortlessly over her head and onto the rough wooden floor. Her previously nervous energy had transformed under Teague's practiced hand, now fueling her need for touch and taste, for more. She stood topless and wanting.

Part of her was shocked at how quickly she had thrown her grand, romantic plan to the wind. After all, hadn't she come to please Teague? To take care of them? To ask them to—

The thought crashed to an abrupt halt when Teague's mouth found Kyle's breasts, tongue teasing and playing. Kyle let out a gasp, her musings tossed aside for the intensity of sensation that Teague was blessing her with. She once again tangled her hands in her lover's long hair, fingers tracing mindless patterns across their scalp as Teague coaxed more and more pleasure from her.

Kyle would worry about the proposal later.

After all, there were more important matters to attend to.

Teague moved back, though only enough to speak, her breath hot and wet against Kyle's chest. "What do you want, Captain?" Teague asked. They stared upward; their deep hazel-green eyes clouded with lust.

"You."

15

3.

Kyle's entire being thrummed with warm contentment. She felt safe, calm, and that she and Teague were the only two people in the world.

From below them, the sound of heavy glass shattering wafted up, followed by a high-pitched screech and a cacophony of laughter.

Well, they were the only two that mattered right then, anyway.

Kyle and Teague lay together on Teague's narrow bed, both thoroughly sated and happy to lounge with each other. Legs a tangled mess, Teague had made themself comfortable on their stomach, head resting on their pillow, which was propped up slightly by their arms beneath it. Their eyes were closed, face calm, the flush from lovemaking still fading. Kyle lay on her side next to them and lightly ran her hand over their exposed back, fingers tracing the rise and fall of their spine with a feather-light touch.

"Mmm…that feels good," Teague murmured, their voice thick with the same tired contentment that Kyle felt.

"That's why I'm doing it." Kyle chuckled softly. This wasn't a sexual touch. Far from it. Kyle had learned that when Teague was stressed or carried tension in their body, a light massage, the barest ghost of a touch, was what worked best to chase the strain away. "I know you had a difficult day."

Teague let out a groan, turning their head to bury their face in the pillow, muffling the sound. "Of all the days for a damned fleet to dock at the bazaar."

"Don't let Nico hear you call it a fleet," Kyle warned. She pushed herself up to sit, straightening her back and affecting her brother's posture. "He'll get all puffed up and argue that it's *little more than a brigand and his band of bullies.*" She tried to feign a caricature of her brother's voice before shaking her head dismissively. Turning onto her back, she stared up at the exposed wooden beams of the ceiling. "I don't know why he gets so out of sorts when it comes to Fairbanks. Leave him alone, and he'll leave you alone."

"Unless he gets a job that involves harassing you," Teague pointed out.

"True," Kyle admitted.

"And your brother is a Sursum Navy man. We all know Sursum has been the most frustrated by Fairbanks and his fleet."

"Band of bullies," Kyle corrected and laughed again. "But you are right."

"Besides, you avoid Fairbanks because you've run afoul of half of his crewmates more than once or twice."

"It was one job. How was I to know that my client had hired more than one privateer?" Kyle huffed. She still smarted over having to give over the fees. It was why she still owed Lamark a favor. He had kept her from losing her ship. Still, she couldn't deny Teague's claim. "But also tru–"

BANG! BANG! BANG!

Both Kyle and Teague startled at the sharp sound of pounding that came from the chamber door.

"What in the water's depths?" Teague gasped under their breath.

"Maybe it's your sister?"

After all, Bess had said she would send up wine and what little food she could spare. This didn't feel like Bess, though. When it came to Teague, Bess was always kind to the point of being taken advantage of. Older sister's prerogative. Bess also would announce herself. So, what then? An overzealous server bringing their food? A belligerent drunk who had taken the wrong stairs?

Teague opened their mouth to call out, but Kyle shook her head, putting a finger to her own lips in a silencing gesture before she quietly climbed out of the bed and to the door. The banging came again, harder, shaking the heavy wood. Kyle knelt down on the floor, checking the space between the bottom of the door and the threshold of the frame. It was barely an inch, but she could see at least two sets of booted feet, maybe three. Nice boots, too.

Nice boots with fine Adalarian designs in the pristine leather.

Dread shot up her spine.

She pushed herself to stand, casting about quickly for her clothing. At Teague's confused expression, Kyle mouthed *Get dressed, now!*

Teague stiffened but did what Kyle said, quietly slipping out of the bed and joining the search for their garments.

On the other side of the door, Kyle could hear muffled conversation.

"Is she even in there?" came one voice, a low bass.

"I heard movement," was the response.

Then the door once again shuddered, whoever was on the other side pounding violently against it in an angry exaggeration of a knock.

Why tonight of all nights?

Kyle could have wept. She snatched her trousers up swiftly, slipping into them and fumbling with the five-button fastening. *Who puts five buttons on trousers?* Her fingers struggled to close them and ensure her pants were securely held at her hips while also scrambling to find the rest of her clothing.

Teague was in a similar state of rush beside her, though with far more grace, sliding effortlessly into breeches that might as well have been painted onto their shapely legs. "What trouble did you bring to my door, Ky? Can we not have one normal evening to ourselves?"

Kyle flinched. It wasn't difficult to hear the frustration in her lover's voice. Worse yet, Kyle couldn't refute this charge, either. They weren't *wrong.* Kyle Talos seemed to have trouble irrevocably lodged in her shadow. The issues with Fairbanks, her plans for proposal falling to bits, all of it. Bad luck liked to follow her. It was something she'd inherited from her father.

Thanks, Da.

"I thought you found it endearing," Kyle quipped, flashing a grin and a wink while inwardly trying to recover some of her pride. She finally obtained victory over her trousers and spotted her blouse and captain's coat where they'd been tossed to the floor beside a nearby chair. "Besides, though I flatter myself saying it, our activities this evening were far better than simply 'normal.' Perhaps even 'breathtaking' or 'spectacular'?"

Teague shot her a cutting look, and Kyle was suddenly feeling less and less like she had *ever* been endearing to her lover. Apparently, though, she looked suitably contrite. Teague's glower faded into a grudging smile. They never could manage to stay mad at Kyle, and Kyle knew it. Counted on it, even.

Teague's softening expression vanished the moment the knocking came again, this time hard enough to shake the door on its hinges.

"Who the hell is looking for you?" they asked, hazel eyes widening with real worry this time.

Kyle shrugged as she yanked her shirt on, jamming the loose fabric into her waistband. She had an inkling, a suspicion, but she also had no desire to remain long enough to have it confirmed or disproven. "Damned if I know, but I don't mean to stay and find out."

"Ah, yes, leave me to clean up the mess," Teague said, though their voice was only half sarcastic. The other half was laden with sadness that gave Kyle pause.

Do they actually think I'm leaving without them?

Kyle hopped on one foot, using both hands to hastily pull on one boot, then switched to do the same with the other. The banging came again. This time, it was more insistent and accompanied by raised voices, shouting to be allowed entrance. It was only a matter of time before they forced the door open. Kyle continued to ignore them for the moment as she grabbed and bundled her belt and coat together in her arms. She moved to the window, which meant standing on the bed, and threw it open. A blast of salty air and fog rushed inside the room, the smell of seafoam and the wet dock coaxing a smile from her. It was the smell of freedom.

This was it. This was the moment to act. Maybe not to propose, but this was the first step. It wasn't how Kyle had imagined the evening progressing, but she could feel that fate was gifting her a moment of dashing romance. She turned back to Teague, who had dressed and was preparing to deal with whoever was on the other side of the door. Mustering her most dashing grin, she asked, "Come with me?"

Teague froze, eyes wide in their beautiful face. "What?"

"Come with me, *vanimelda*," Kyle repeated, the Adalarian term of endearment rolling off of her tongue as she stretched a hand out in invitation.

Teague studied Kyle, then glanced back around the small room, taking everything in. Understanding in their eyes told Kyle that Teague comprehended the invitation wasn't just for a romp, that it was something far bigger, far more important. Of course, it wasn't entirely fair to spring it on them with an unknown danger on the other side of the door. A storm of confusion, hesitance, and even fear passed over Teague's features as they tried to make this decision.

The door once again shook on its hinges, the metal creaking under the strain of the now continuous knocking and banging. Kyle didn't think they were just knocking now. Now, they were going to force their way in. The sound of splintering wood sliced across the quarters, making Teague's decision for them. "Gods damn it," they breathed, reaching out to take Kyle's outstretched hand. "You had better keep me safe."

"Of course," Kyle promised and meant it.

It was easy for the ship captain to slip out of the window and onto the roof of the inn, and she helped Teague down after her, making sure her grip on her lover's waist was steady. "Don't worry," Kyle whispered, placing a quick kiss on their cheek. "I'll be your big, strong pirate," she teased, reaching up to close the window behind them.

"Short, strong pirate," Teague corrected, but their smile was warm and confident.

"Nuance."

A crash and heavy boom of the door finally giving way arose from the room they'd just escaped from, and it was all the encouragement the two needed to continue their getaway.

As swiftly as she dared, Kyle guided her companion across the roof, crouching to avoid the two other dormers on the cramped building's third floor. They were on the second-floor roof and no doubt the patrons in the rooms below could hear them scurrying across. The slate tiles beneath her feet weren't her first choice in safe surfaces to walk on, but the escaping couple didn't suffer too much slipping before making it to the far end of the roof. It dropped off, but not far, as the roof of the first floor, the tavern itself, extended to the front.

Kyle lowered Teague down to the first-floor roof, then followed, both of them hastening to the edge of the building with all the stealth they could manage. When they reached the edge, they repeated the same process, finally finding themselves on the slatted docks that constituted the narrow alley between the *Port in the Storm* and the neighboring building, another inn. The alley itself was cramped, barely fitting the two of them standing side by side, and seawater splashed up in small droplets between the damp slats of wood.

The air around them smelled of grilled meat, seaweed, and stale spirits. All the things Kyle would expect from the Bazaar on its best and worst nights. That was the beauty of Saltskiff; half of the time, one couldn't tell its finest from its least. Slipping towards the front of the alley, Kyle peeked out. It was late, yet the dock was still packed with people. The line to get into *Port in the Storm* wasn't as long as it had been, but there were more than enough people milling about to form a crowd. Kyle grinned. She and Teague would be practically home free once they slipped into the ebb and flow of faces.

As if cued by her thoughts and intent on ruining her plans, she could hear the pounding of feet from inside *Port in the Storm*. Shouts and disgruntled bellows accompanied by the hard clatter of boots on rickety wood heading towards the front from within clued Kyle in on the swiftly dwindling time to escape. Whoever had broken into Teague's room had obviously found it empty and come down much faster than Kyle had expected.

Kyle peered around the side of the building just in time to see the front door thrown open. Two men dressed in the colors of the Adalarian lands stepped out, their eyes immediately searching. Kyle ducked back into the safety of the shadowed alley. It would be too risky to try and slip out in full view of the entryway to the tavern, even with the crowds still moving over the docks.

So much for home free.

Kyle shrank back into the shadows of the alley, her hand moving to find Teague's. When she did, she tugged gently and nodded in the direction that sank deeper into the darkness of the alley. "This way."

"Kyle Talos, if you get me killed…" they said, warning in their voice.

Kyle had to wince. When Teague used her full name, she knew she was in trouble. "Don't worry," she tried to assure them. "We will be fine."

4.

The western docks of the Bazaar were quiet by design. While the area was teeming with people during the day, the Saltskiff founders deliberately made it so taverns and inns had no place there. This way, there would be room enough for all of the comings and goings of the sailor folk. The dock on the northern side of the Bazaar operated in the same way. Both were set up as administrative centers: port fees, merchandise exchange or delivery, ship repairs, and booking passage on a ship were the businesses of the docks, and everyone else had to fulfill other needs elsewhere. It meant that, once sunset came and most offices closed, a peace descended on the docks that nowhere else in the Bazaar could boast of. Only the port fees office remained open, and the local community guard patrolled the docks to keep crime to a minimum. Part of the port fees Kyle always planned on was an extra coin or two to the community guard to make sure *The Stargazer* was just a bit safer than it might otherwise be.

Confident that they had slipped away from the pursuers, Kyle felt comfortable enough to leave the comparative safety of the shadowed alley. She and Teague had taken the winding route from the Silvermoon district, slipping in and out of the narrow spaces between buildings and converted ships, the wood bobbing and swaying more so than the rest of the city. While the main thoroughfares were well maintained, their bindings tightened and replaced regularly, the byways were less so. The wood dipped and swayed, and both Kyle and Teague were soaked to the knees. Still, they were safe, and that was something.

Checking to make sure their pursuers were gone, Kyle reached back for Teague's hand. "I told you I would keep us safe," she said, leading them out of the alley.

"Mmhmm," Teague agreed begrudgingly. They were obviously uncomfortable with the escape and hugged themself in the moonlight, shivering.

"How are you?" Kyle asked.

Teague shrugged and hummed a frustratingly neutral sound as they ran their hands up and down their arms, trying to warm themself.

Kyle huffed, glancing up and down the street. She was trying not to take out her frustration on Teague's reticence. The plans for the night had been ruined, and for whatever reason, there were well-dressed Adalarian soldiers who were aggressively seeking at least a word with her. If all of that wasn't bad enough, Kyle could feel Teague closing up, as they sometimes did when stressed or overwrought. While Teague had never come out and admitted it, Kyle could easily see it was a defense mechanism. If one became impenetrable, they could avoid being hurt.

Except they also avoided things like honest discussions and emotional sharing, two things Kyle thought vital in a relationship. It was all the ship's captain could do not to throw her hands in the air in frustration.

This entire night was turning out to be cursed.

Instead, Kyle shrugged out of her brocade captain's coat, offering it to them.

"It won't fit," Teague said flatly.

At least they had finally spoken. "Praise the waters! Your voice hasn't left you," Kyle jested, grinning. She stepped forward and placed the coat on Teague's shoulders, more a shawl than anything else. "It is something and should offer some warmth. Come. Soon, we will be safely aboard *The Stargazer*, with dry clothes and soft, thick blankets to chase off the cold."

"And then what?" Teague clutched at the edges of the coat, pulling it tighter around their shoulders.

"Nico and Da are both aboard. I'll talk it over with them and get their thoughts," she explained.

"And then?" Teague pressed. They did not like being unsure of a plan. Their voice was thin, stretched taut with tension.

Kyle paused for a moment, considering the question. In truth, she hadn't given much thought to the 'what comes next' aspect of the evening. She had just gone into action. She had perceived danger, or at least the possibility of danger, and fallen back on *The Stargazer* being her safe place. It had been so since her childhood, since before it was hers. "We can lay low in the ship tonight. In the morning, we will head back to *Port in the Storm* and see what, if any, damage was done."

"Y-You don't think they would do anything to Bess or Arthur, do you?" they asked. Their voice wavered, lower lip trembling with the threat of tears.

Kyle hadn't considered that, but once the possibility was presented, her answer was immediate and firm. "No. It would stir up too much trouble, especially when *Port in the Storm* is filled with patrons. Bess and Arthur have the security of numbers and allies." Kyle moved closer and put her arms around Teague's waist. "Your siblings are safe. I'm sure of it. And we will be once we've reached *The Stargazer*."

Reluctantly, Teague nodded. They blinked away their tears and let out a long breath before wrapping Kyle in a hug. The two of them stayed there for a moment, taking in that brief calm, before separating. Teague took Kyle's hand, gave it an affectionate squeeze, and nodded for her to lead on.

Kyle felt the weight of her love's trust and tried not to let its warmth be chilled with guilt. After all, none of this would have happened had Kyle not been followed. Whether she knew those following her or why they were seeking her out was irrelevant. She had laid this trouble at Teague's door, and it gnawed at her.

Turning towards the arched entryway to the docks, she made sure to be vigilant with each step. At the gate, a single Saltskiff guard stopped the two of them, asking for identification.

"Kyle Talos," she explained, stepping forward to hand over a small leatherbound book. It was her personal port ledger, serving as a record of every town *The Stargazer* had dropped anchor in. It was a requirement at most ports, and while Saltskiff didn't strictly require the record, it went a long way to assuaging the suspicion of the guards. They liked to know who was coming and going.

"Leaving port?" the guard asked, raising a suspicious eyebrow.

"No, just returning to my ship. All fees are paid through the eight-day."

The guard took the most cursory glance at the ledger then handed it back. He dismissed them with a curt "Move along."

Kyle did not need to be told twice.

The humid night air around them smelled of salt water and mildew, an inescapable mix so close to the open water. Still, once aboard the ship, it would be the scents of warm wood, fresh clothing, and the soft comforts of blankets and a bed. Luckily for the two of them, *The Stargazer* had nabbed a prime spot when putting into port. They did not have far to walk before they reached the vessel.

Kyle wasn't overly surprised to find that the gangplank had been pulled away, and there was no easy way to access her ship. More than likely, her father or brother had brought it aboard to deter anyone from simply traipsing onto the ship. It was yet another security measure when one docked. Of course, as most security measures did, it only served to frustrate Kyle just then.

"Cover your ears," she warned Teague.

Kyle stepped back as far as she could without falling off the other side of the pier, hoping to get a better look up to the deck of her ship. She put two fingers into her mouth and let out a shrill whistle. She did this in two short bursts, then one long, sustained note. The two-and-one whistle was something her father had done for years. Nico and Kyle had grown up with this whistle. It was one of the surest ways to get their attention while letting them know it was her. Another benefit?

It was so loud it would raise the dead if such a thing were possible.

After all, how else did one alert their children among rowdy shiphands or busy docks? Kyle swore that whistle could be heard for miles. Whenever she and Nico had heard it as children, they knew it was time to return to their father.

Kyle cupped her hands around her mouth so that her shout carried when she called. "Ahoy there! Nico? Da? Someone drop the plank so we can come aboard."

There was a silence following her call. For a moment, she wasn't sure she'd been heard. She expected to hear a return shout and some insult about her being obnoxious, but there was nothing. She was about to give another whistle when she heard shuffling. The gangplank was lowered, and Kyle offered Teague another grin. "Your chariot, my liege."

"You are ridiculous, you know that?" they replied, but they were smiling. A mix of trepidation and exhaustion lined their face, but there was relief as well. They approached the gangway and hurried delicately up and onto the ship.

Kyle breathed a small sigh, feeling a bit easier now that they had made it to *The Stargazer*. Not only had she led them on a successful escape from whoever had been pursuing them, but it seemed that she had assuaged Teague's foul mood, at least to some degree. She wanted to make sure they were completely at ease, and there was a clear plan in place to check that all was right with Teague's family before anything else was addressed.

Very few people agreed to marriage when upset and concerned about their other loved ones.

Kyle strode up the gangplank and onto the sturdy decking of *The Stargazer*, finding herself just behind Teague.

Teague stood ramrod straight, and when Kyle put a hand against their back in a gentle encouragement to get them to move forward, they did not budge. They were frozen, muscles tense.

Behind Kyle, the gangway vanished, the wood clattering on the dock below before a roughened splash told her that it had plunged into the dark waters.

Not good.

Acting without thinking, Kyle moved swiftly, placing herself in front of Teague and between them and whatever threat had found the two of them.

Four guards, weapons drawn, had them pinned to the railing of the ship. Adalarian guards, with their fine leather armor, exactly like the

27

design on the boots Kyle had seen back in Teague's room. Kyle felt her heart sink. She and Teague were effectively surrounded. Kyle recognized the arms emblazoned on the enemy's garments as well. The deep sage green and silver inlay of the Sixth Court of Elders for the kingdom of Adalar.

Her deceased mother's homeland.

Kyle dropped into a ready stance. Perhaps, if she could wrestle a weapon from one of them, she could distract them long enough for Teague to escape. She knew her lover could swim, and perhaps it would keep her from—

A loud, authoritative, and chillingly familiar voice interrupted Kyle's plan to attack. "Yield, or the guards will force you to."

"This is no way to treat a captain aboard her own ship," quipped Kyle, hot anger now mixing with the adrenaline that had been coursing through her.

Moving behind the guards, Kyle caught sight of a tall, elegant Adalarian woman. She was obviously in charge of the guards. Her pale, silvery hair was long, pulled back in a single braid that lay over one haughty shoulder. Sharp, gray eyes cut across Kyle, and Kyle had no doubts that if the woman could, she would kill her with that glare. Next to the Adalarian woman stood a slightly shorter woman, also Adalarian. This one was younger. Her hair was cut short, close-cropped, and neatly combed against her head. This one looked decidedly more upset than the older, more elegant counterpart, eyes darting between Kyle and the taller woman.

"Yield, *brinmeltyth*," ordered the leader. She offered a sneer with the Adalarian insult.

Kyle rolled her eyes, being sure the older woman saw the expression. If only they knew the number of times Kyle had had to deal with uptight Adalarians using 'half-blood' as an insult. Xenophobic blowhards, all of them. Still, Kyle wasn't without fear of this woman, and she straightened, holding her hands up in a gesture of surrender as icy dread slid down her spine. She refused to show it, though. "*Irfenrihen,*" she said, addressing the Adalarian leader with an insult of her own. Turnabout being fair play and all of that.

The Adalarian woman's countenance lost its smugness to a flicker of outrage. When she spoke again, she no longer used Adalarian. "How dare you address me in such a manner?"

"How dare you attack me on my own ship?"

She scoffed. "I shouldn't have to deal with such filth."

Kyle shrugged. "Neither should I."

From behind her, Teague whispered nervously, "What in the depths is going on here, Ky?" They were holding tightly to the back of Kyle's shirt, and she could tell they were steeping in anxiety.

She wasn't sure the 'what,' but she could sure as hell speak to the 'who' of the situation. "Teague, this is Vána Raudnost of the Sixth Court of Adalarian Elders. She is my mother's mother." Kyle was trying to keep her tone light and unworried. She didn't want to panic Teague. "The woman next to her is my aunt, Valeria Raudnost, also of the Sixth Court," she explained, indicating to the woman standing beside Vána. "Great Aunt, Vána, this is my partner, Teague Dailann."

"A pleasure," murmured Teague, their voice expressing precisely zero pleasure.

"*Silence!*" Vána all but spat. She moved to stand beside the guards. Their weapons were still drawn and ready for a command to attack. With a gesture from her, they lowered them but didn't sheath them. "I'm glad we came here. It seems my men did not find you at the inn, but there were few places for you to go once flushed out from that…" she trailed off, looking for the right word. "*Establishment*," she said finally, the word dripping with contempt.

Teague shifted behind Kyle, their grip on Kyle's shirt tightening ever so slightly. Still, they were wise enough to hold their tongue.

"Why are you here?" Kyle asked through gritted teeth.

Vána took a deep, slow breath, a calmness smoothing away the disdain from her face. "I need you to take me somewhere. In return, I am giving you an opportunity to be part of a glorious journey and share in all of the fruits of one of the most historical discoveries of our time. You and I, Kalina, will lead—"

Kyle winced at the sound of her Adalarian name. She had left it in the past when her mother died, and her relations showed no interest in her, and to hear it again after all this time was jarring. "Kyle," she snapped, interrupting her progenitor's speech.

Vána started at the interruption. "Excuse me?"

"My name is Kyle."

Vána froze for just a moment, and a twitch of the muscle just above her left eye was the only indication of any emotion, but Kyle had learned long ago that it was Vána's rage, and it was terrifying. Kyle swallowed and hoped she didn't look as worried as she felt.

"Whatever you call yourself means little to me," Vána said. "Your Adalarian name is Kalina, and that is what I shall use when addressing you." The grandeur of her words had vanished, apparently ruined by the interruption. She was all business now, steely eyes cold. "You are going to take me and mine to the Elysium Cove."

Kyle couldn't have been more surprised if her mother's mother had asked to go to one of the many moons of a far-off planet. She scoffed, stopping just short of outright laughing at the woman's words. "Me? What would you want with a small-time, *half-blood* family embarrassment when a word from the great Vána Raudnost can command the fleets of the Adalarian navy?" she asked.

Teague clenched Kyle's shirt hard, twisting it in warning. Kyle had to remember that she wasn't alone and was already pushing her luck. Riling up a member of the higher Adalarian echelons of society and political strategies might not be the best course at that or any moment. Still, Kyle was having difficulty keeping her emotions in check.

"My reasons are my ow—"

"Oh no, no, they are not," Kyle argued. She shook her head vehemently. "Not when you're trying to forcibly commandeer my ship."

"How dare you speak to me with such disrespect!" Vána hissed, practically baring her teeth as she spat the words. Her eyes blazed with anger, but Kyle thought it was covering something else, something more than just outrage.

Something like hesitation.

Hesitating about what?

"She came to the Bazaar for respect?" Teague whispered the question, their breath warm against Kyle's ear.

Kyle had to admit the point. But why *was* Vána here? Why attempt to commandeer a ship like *The Stargazer* when one had the force of the Adalarian Navy at one's command? It made no sense.

Unless she doesn't have the authority to requisition the ships...

Realization slowly dawned on Kyle, and she stared at Vána. This woman was from a noble family and was a respected member of the highest court in Adalar, a country that prided itself on proper decorum. Could she be disobeying the Courts she thought so highly of? The possibility defied everything she knew of Vána, and yet Kyle had no other explanation for the behavior. "You don't have their blessing, do you?" she asked slowly, the words deliberate.

Vána glared at her but remained silent.

The refusal to answer emboldened Kyle, and she gave a short, amazed laugh. "The Courts refused a venture to the Elysium Cove, didn't they? Or do they even know?"

Kyle barely finished speaking before Vána stepped forward, seething. Her hand was around Kyle's throat in an instant, and she squeezed hard. Teague gave out a shout, Vána's advance pushing them back hard against the railing. Kyle was stuck between her grandmother's attack and her lover.

She grabbed Vána's arm, choking out her words. "Why would you be going there, *grandmother?*" Kyle made the title sound more like a slur than a statement of fact. It was the only way she could ever stomach the truth of it. "Are you seeking the Well of Eternal Life without the blessing of the courts? After all, that's all that's out there, unless you seek your death in the storm.".

Vána, as if realizing she had allowed her anger to run roughshod over her actions, released her granddaughter. Turning, she moved to put some distance between them before looking back. Her face was smooth again, composure regained, but her gaze was hard with anger and determination. "I am doing what those fools are afraid to do. The Seven Courts will thank me when all is said and done."

Kyle coughed hard once she was freed, her throat burning. Teague helped to steady her, keeping them both upright. Kyle could feel the small crescent cuts in her neck where Vána's nails had dug in. The captain took a moment to suck in air and clear her throat before she tried to speak, hoping her voice would not desert her. "If the Court refused you, what makes you think I would agree?" she asked, trying to sound more confident than she felt.

Whatever the answer, Kyle knew as soon as Vána's face settled into a calm, serenely smug expression. She felt her gut tighten as Vána gestured to one of the guards surrounding Kyle and Tague. The soldier nodded and moved, striding to the stairs and vanishing below deck.

A tense, almost awkward silence fell between everyone on deck.

"Are you all right?" whispered Teague. Their voice was barely audible to even Kyle.

"I am," was Kyle's response. Dread and anticipation swirled in her gut as she tried to figure out just what Vána had in store for them. For the first time since the exchange had begun, Kyle turned her eyes to Valeria. Her aunt, who had been looking on her with a mixture of sympathy and worry, now avoided her gaze, her pallor increasing under Kyle's scrutiny. It only made Kyle's foreboding worse.

The sound of the soldier's return could be heard. Not only that, but there was more. A strange commotion of grunts, shuffling, and even dragging. As if the guard brought someone who was constantly faltering and sliding.

It wasn't the guard that appeared first on the steps. Instead, someone was thrown upwards, unable to check their momentum. They tripped on the top step and landed in a heap on the deck. It was an older man, face gaunt and half covered in blood.

Kyle recognized him immediately.

Phaiden Talos was a man who had just moved from his late fifties into his sixtieth year of life, not that any man or woman would be able to guess it. He had the appearance and vigor of a man ten years younger, his handsome face a warm tan, his groomed beard and hair peppered with silver among the darker strands of gray and black. He usually wore a roguish grin and a smile in his eyes, but now he was beaten and bruised, the white of one eye turned crimson by blood from a gash just above it. His hands were bound behind his back, and he had nothing to break his fall when he landed on the sturdy wood of the ship's deck.

"Da!" she shouted, moving forward.

"Kyle..." he groaned, trying to right himself. The guard that had brought him up put a foot to Phaiden's back, forcing him down against the wood.

One of the guards closest to Kyle shot out a hand to stop her. Without slowing, she took it and twisted it hard, bringing his arm up around his back and pressing upwards mercilessly. She felt the shoulder pop out of place just before the soldier cried his pain. She put a foot in front of his and shoved forward, eliciting another pained yell from him as he fell to the deck. Before she could grab for his weapons, though, the tip of a blade hit the tender flesh of her throat, and she froze.

Vána's icy gaze met Kyle's over the metal of the thin sword. She smiled without mirth. "I did worse to the other one. He should have stopped resisting."

The other one? Nico?

Kyle's eyes narrowed as she stared at the hateful woman. For the first time that evening, true panic coursed through her, raw and incapacitating. Had she killed Nico? No. No, she wouldn't have. Not because Vána wasn't capable of it, but because she knew Kyle wouldn't help her if any of her father's side had been slain.

But it was often surprising what one might live through.

Kyle swallowed against the blade at her throat and felt it bob with the movement.

"Now, you will take me and my soldiers to the Elysium Cove. We will break through the storm, and I will get everything I have coming to me."

"How?" Kyle breathed the word through gritted teeth.

"With this." With her unoccupied hand, Vána withdrew a necklace from beneath her clothing. It was a silver chain that held it around her neck, and at the end was a pale blue pendant that glistened in the starlight. "This will get us safely through the storm." She canted her head to the side, voice betraying the enjoyment she was now taking from Kyle's current position. "If you do not agree, I will kill your father, brother, and partner, and then you, take your ship and leave your bodies to rot with the rest of the refuse in this disgusting place. Do you understand?"

Kyle's jaw tightened. She had no choice but to acquiesce, and she nodded her assent.

"I did not hear you, Kalina," Vána snapped, applying just a little pressure to her blade.

"I understand," Kyle ground out.

"Good," Vána replied. She withdrew her sword, slid it into the sheath and turned to her soldiers. "Pull anchor. We sail for the Elysium Cove."

5.

Steadily simmering rage flowed through Kyle's veins as Valeria led them below decks, each step of the stairs making the indignation she felt all the hotter and closer to the surface.

This is my ship. They have some damned nerve.

Teague followed silently behind Kyle, keeping a strong hold on her hand. After them, a guard drove a limping Phaiden along. Kyle's father would groan and gasp in pain as he stumbled forward, and it took everything for Kyle not to turn and attack the guard, to do something, anything, in order to defend Phaiden.

Not yet.

She knew that playing along with Vána, waiting for an opportunity to strike, was the best course of action. It would keep them all safer. Still, it didn't lighten the burden of the takeover of her ship, the danger they were in, or being forced to listen to her father's pain. Swallowing frustration and anger was a difficult task for Kyle. She'd been raised as a free spirit, and free spirits tended to indulge their feelings, not to stifle them. The added threat against her loved ones made it all the more galling for Kyle to have to still her hand.

Only a couple of hours earlier, she had been making love to Teague and thinking of marrying the person she adored with every part of her being. Now they were both prisoners on a ship commandeered by the matriarch of Kyle's damned Adalarian family.

Not a shining example of a marriage proposal.

Kyle drove the selfish thought from her mind, attempting to do the same with her anger and frustration. Figuring out an escape from the situation in one piece was more important. She needed to ascertain the severity of her brother's and father's injuries. The next task would be getting Vána and her guard off of the ship and leading her loved ones and herself to safety.

She knew that Vána wouldn't hesitate to put down any true sign of rebellion against her venture. Without Adalarian council approval, she would need the most loyal soldiers to attempt something as extreme as what she was doing. More than one sneer or dirty look from a guard made Kyle think they might even be Adalarian supremacists, which meant a whole other level of elitism. After all, the odds were that Vána would seek out those who would be viciously loyal. That meant they needed more than your average guard. Given all of that, Kyle was rather surprised Vána hadn't just stolen the damn ship. Perhaps killing Nico and Phaiden and making off would draw too much attention. Or maybe having the captain of the vessel along would help to explain why a ship not flying the colors of the Sixth Court had two of its highest-ranking members aboard.

Regardless of the reasoning, Kyle wasn't about to sit idle while her ancestress sailed them headlong into death. The eternally churning storms that wreathed the Elysium Cove would rip *The Stargazer* to shreds before any of her crew saw the sand of its cursed beaches. Many greater and more heavily armored ships had been beaten to splinter. Hers would be no different.

Just the thought brought tears to her eyes as Valeria led them down the stairs from the main deck. As the smell of night air and seawater made way for the warm, damp scent of the ship's timber, the very thought of possibly losing *The Stargazer* filled her with dread. Kyle *had* to think of something before it went that far.

She knew her ship better than any living soul aside from her father and brother. She and Nico had spent their childhood aboard, and the intimate knowledge could give Kyle some advantage that Vána and her troops didn't have. One she hoped she could exploit.

One she had yet to come up with.

Kyle quietly counted the four guards stationed on the gundeck, making note of where they were positioned as Valeria led them along the length of the deck. They were all dressed in the pristine colors of the Sixth Court, and all except one were making an effort not to look at Valeria's little group as they strode by the cannons. As its name implied, the gundeck held the majority of *The Stargazer's* cannons, which numbered ten below deck and six above. It was also where much of the crew most often slept, either on cots or in hammocks slung above the cannons and other accoutrements of the ship. Oh, there were perfectly fine quarters on the ship for her crew, but they preferred to leave them for passengers, or anyone else they jested was too weak to handle the life of a privateer.

None of her crew's belongings, the few they kept out, had been touched. Kyle was oddly comforted by that.

Valeria took the second set of stairs *The Stargazer* boasted, at the other end of the deck. She ushered the small group down again, this time to the orlop deck. A bit more cramped, this was mostly for cable, sail, and carpentry stores, though it housed more than just storage. Beyond that was the galley, an area for livestock on the rare occasions there was any to transport, and the infirmary, which was a moderate space that Kyle was always sure to keep well-stocked despite the surprising fact that the crew made little use of it.

There were another four guards on the orlop deck and one extra standing at the doorway to the infirmary. The knot in Kyle's gut tightened as they wove through the storage and ropes running along the deck and came to the sick room.

"We've come to see the other one," Valeria said. Her voice was quiet and kept carefully neutral. "And to bring this one back." She gestured vaguely in Phaiden's direction.

This was the first time that Kyle had heard that voice in years. After all, it had been nearly sixteen summers since Kyle's mother, Meliandra, had passed away. Kyle hadn't seen her aunt since. She had forgotten how deep and rich her voice was, and the reminder conjured a memory in Kyle's mind's eye. It was one of countless evenings where Valeria and Meliandra would share a bottle of strong wine and laugh at the stories each told. Kyle had been too young to really remember what their jokes and stories had been about, but she clearly remembered the full-throated, unabashed laughter, as if neither Meliandra nor Valeria had a care as to who might overhear. It was a bright, happy memory.

37

Kyle was surprised she had any of those left of her mother's side of the family.

The guard moved aside at the order, allowing the small group entry.

Valeria turned and faced Kyle. She somehow managed to meet her niece's gaze, and her expression was one of thinly veiled remorse. She gestured to the door. "You may enter and visit, but only briefly." She addressed the guard with her next instruction, saying, "They are allowed without your presence in the room but remain by the door. They will not be staying here for long, and I will return shortly for them. The only ones to stay are the healer and the two injured men."

"Yes, ma'am."

"Call me if there is trouble," she added, almost as an afterthought.

"At once, ma'am."

Valeria caught Kyle's eye, the look on her face speaking of warning and concern. *Don't make waves,* it silently said. *Please.* Then she strode off.

Teague gave Kyle's hand a squeeze in support, and the two of them went into the infirmary.

"What now?" came a sharp, nasal voice.

Before Kyle had taken two steps into the space, an Adalarian man of roughly her own height stood to block her path. His long, dark hair was pulled neatly back in a braid that ran from the crown of his head down to his shoulder blades. The expression of his elegant features was fierce, and he looked ready to do battle. He stopped when he realized that she wasn't a guard. Looking past Kyle and Teague, he spotted the guard dragging Phaiden and let out a huff. "Sorry," he curtly offered to Kyle. "I thought you were *someone else.*" As he spoke, he glared daggers at the guard. It was clear that he had no love for the man posted at the door. Kyle wondered if it was just this one or all of them. If so, perhaps *that* was something she might use.

Perhaps they both disliked Vána and her guard and could find common ground.

Beyond the dark-haired man, Kyle saw that one of the four cots of the infirmary was occupied. Nico lay so deathly still on the closest one, his head lolling to one side. She thought for an instant that he was dead and tears stung her eyes. But no. The rise and fall of his chest was slow, and in the quiet, she could hear the shallow wheezing of his breath. His face was mottled and bruised, clear indicators of the beating he had taken, one that looked worse than his father's. Deep gashes on his cheek and across his forehead had been sutured, though they were red and angry. His arm rested over a thin, clean blanket that covered most of him, though his left arm was splinted and the skin she could see around the splint was swollen and discolored. The bone was probably broken.

Her vision ran red with outrage as she watched her older brother struggle for breath. She couldn't see any other injuries, but she knew, she just *knew* they were there. Her entire body contracted, stiffening as wrath washed over her. Who in the depths did Vána think she was?

"Kyle?" whispered Teague, voice pained. "Kyle, you're hurting me."

Teague's words brought Kyle out of her fury. Without realizing, she had been squeezing their hand hard enough to bruise. She quickly dropped it, guilt coloring her face. "Sorry."

However, Teague snatched Kyle's hand and readjusted their hold. "There," they said and gave Kyle's hand a firm squeeze. "I'm here."

Kyle took a breath, relieved, and felt herself relax just a fraction.

"I understand this is jarring," the dark-haired man said. It sounded very much like the beginning of an apology, but before he could finish whatever he was trying to say, he was shouldered rather rudely by the guard who dragged Kyle's father in, hefting him onto a vacant cot like a sack of garbage.

Phaiden's head hit the wooden frame with a solid *thwack*. He groaned, eyelids fluttering slightly before closing. His face paled and he looked stricken in the lantern light of the infirmary.

Kyle was at his side in an instant.

Her quick movements alarmed the guard at the door and the one who had so unceremoniously dropped her father on the cot. Both of the men drew their swords, training them on Kyle's back.

Teague gasped. Kyle, on her knees beside her father, froze.

"Put those away. She is only going to check on the victim of your incompetence," snapped the dark-haired man. His voice was pure impatience. "It's her father that you dropped like some sack of potatoes."

After a moment's hesitation, the guards sheathed their weapons. Not quickly enough, it seemed, for the dark-haired man, whom Kyle was liking more and more with each passing minute. "You're rakefires, the both of you. Get out," he shouted. "Get out!"

Both guards obeyed the order, though did not look pleased about it. Slowly they sheathed their steel, cool gazes moving around the infirmary. The taller of the two nodded to the shorter, then strode out. The shorter, the guard that would remain, left after, and shut the door behind him. Even with the infirmary being free from guards, Kyle remembered Valaria's orders. The men might be gone from the room, but they were still listening.

The dark-haired man huffed loudly, then began again, his voice at half the volume as it had been. "As I was saying, I know this must be very jarring. Believe me, I am as disgusted as I could be. I did not join with this crew to steal and injure." He offered a small nod. "I'm called Ioan. I am the healer that was deceived into this godsforsaken journey." He didn't quite smile, but he was no longer frowning, and that appeared to be a step in the right direction.

"Deceived?" Teague echoed.

Ioan scoffed. "Most apothecaries and healers try to ease suffering, not travel with those who would inflict it."

"Then why?"

"See more of Theia? Enjoy the pay? Not be engaged to whatever individual with a large fortune my parents might attempt to stick me with?" he offered. "Take your pick."

Kyle blinked up at him. She was having some issue shifting from the standoffish disregard of the Adalarian soldiers they had passed to the conversational tone that this new acquaintance was taking. "We don't know you. We don't trust you," she said. She wasn't sure if she made the statement to remind herself of that.

He thought on that for a moment, then shrugged. "Good point." He moved to kneel down next to Kyle, gesturing towards her father. "May I at least resituate and examine him?"

Kyle nodded her assent slowly.

At her acquiescence, Ioan took careful hold of Phaiden's legs and lifted them, gently readjusting the unconscious man so that he lay entirely and comfortably on the cot. Reaching past Kyle, Ioan put a hand to Phaiden's throat, feeling for a pulse. Satisfied, he moved again, feeling the man's forehead, careful to avoid the injured skin. He lifted each eyelid with a thumb to examine the irises. After a quiet moment, he nodded. "I feel he is stable for now. The wound on his forehead isn't bad, but cuts like that tend to bleed a lot. I will get him cleaned up and make sure he rests."

"And him?" Kyle asked, voice cracking when she pointed to her brother. She didn't want to allow her defenses to fall. She was wary of trusting Ioan, but a small part of her found hope in the possibility of having an ally on the ship. It loosened the hold over her emotions more than she would like. "Will Nico be all right?"

Confusion knit Ioan's brow, then it smoothed as he glanced over to the second occupied cot. "The other one? He is very banged up. I have never seen a man fight so viciously. He's military, isn't he?" Not waiting for a reply, he continued. "They broke his arm, and he lost a lot of blood from a cut on his thigh and a wound on his side. I was able to staunch the flow and suture the injuries, and he is doing well now. I had to give him a draught for pain, and *that* was no easy task. I swear the man thought I was poisoning him."

Kyle chuckled softly. "He was never good at taking medicine."

Ioan offered a small smile. His shoulders had relaxed throughout their exchange, and now he folded his arms over his chest. "Were I his physician, I would recommend at least two weeks' worth of bed rest, then a careful and gradual return to regular duties."

"Do you not know healing magic?" asked Teague.

Kyle was glad there was someone else there to help ask questions. She was such a mix of anger and guilt and fear that there were only so many logical queries she could manage.

"Alas, no. In fact, I suspect that is the reason I am here." At the look of confusion Teague gave him, he continued. "Those skilled in magic, even just healing arts, are more difficult to control." He punctuated the statement with a meaningful glance at the door.

41

"All right," Kyle said. She decided to pin at least some hope on Ioan's words. She had to trust someone, though she would stay on her guard. She generally felt herself a good judge of character, and while the man might be cranky and disgruntled towards the crew, he took his place as healer seriously.

"I'm Kyle." She stood and moved away, back to Teague, who had lowered themselves on an empty cot at the end of the narrow room.

They looked pale. Kyle was sure she did as well. Seating herself down beside Teague, she interwove her fingers in her lover's, a quiet sigh escaping her. "This is my partner, Teague." She introduced them without looking away from their face, searching their eyes for she didn't know what. Perhaps it was only for the comfort of their presence. She discovered Teague looking to her for much the same.

"Pleasure," Ioan offered. "As much as it can be, under these circumstances."

Finally tearing her gaze away from Teague, she turned to Ioan. She wanted to say more, to ask more questions of him, but a knock came at the door. Not overly hard, but insistent.

Ioan dropped his voice to a whisper. "Know that not everyone on this ship supports what Vána has done or intends to do. While I cannot promise much, I am no fighter, I can promise that I am a damn good healer and will guard these men against further injury or harm as well as I am able," he explained in a rushed sibilance.

Almost as soon as he finished, the door swung open, and Valeria stood framed in the open space. Her face was unreadable except for her eyes, which glittered with worry. She looked from Ioan to Kyle and Teague. "You two, follow me. I'll take you to your temporary quarters."

"I can only assume they aren't my rightful captain's quarters?" Kyle asked snappishly.

"No, they are not," came the even answer.

As Kyle and Teague stood and followed Valeria back out of the infirmary, Ioan gave them both a small nod, wordlessly reaffirming his hurried words before he moved to close the door behind them.

Kyle stiffened at the sound of the door clicking shut. She imagined that it held a frightening finality to it.

"I'm here," Teague murmured again, their voice so soft that Kyle almost missed the words.

Kyle nodded but made no other gesture. Her mind was too busy, trying to dismiss her feelings of dread about her father and brother, her guilt at bringing Teague into all of this, and her frustration at not yet having thought up some dashing escape plan for them all. Perhaps they weren't reasonable thoughts, but fatigue was wearing on her and she could not shut them out.

"This is where you will be sleeping."

Valeria's voice snapped Kyle from her inner torments, and she found that they were in the storage room normally kept for the carpentry stores. A single, dim lantern hung from the ceiling, casting smaller piles of scrap wood and board in the shadows that swayed with the subtle movement of the boat. Two hammocks were hung in the corner, out of view of the hallway. It afforded some privacy but given that the carpentry storeroom didn't have a door it was, at best, a small consolation.

There were certainly safer places to sleep on the ship, ones where one didn't have to worry about a stray nail or hammer, but it was dry and that was something.

"These are your quarters for now," Valeria explained.

"Glamorous," Kyle managed.

Valeria let out a long breath and turned, moving back towards the hall. She stopped, checked that there were no guards nearby, and when satisfied, laid a hand on Kyle's shoulder. She leaned in close and breathed her words. "Don't worry. I am sure I can talk my mother out of this."

Kyle didn't answer, only waited for her to continue. Could her aunt be an ally?

"Surely, with a little luck, she will see the error of her ways and we can put this all behind us. We will return your boat and journey back home."

"With a little luck?" Kyle repeated, incredulous. "Valeria, I do not think 'luck' is going to be in play here. We need to *do* something."

"And I will. The closer we get to the Elysium Cove, the more Vána will see reason, I'm sure of it."

"None of this seems very reasonable."

43

Valeria again glanced down the hall. She spoke again, this time in an even lower whisper. "Trust me, Kyle. I will take care of everything."

Kyle stared at her aunt. "What have you seen that makes you think that?"

Her aunt's features darkened, and she huffed her annoyance at Kyle's disbelief. "Just give me a little time." With those final words, she left them, vanishing into the hallway, the sound of her boots on the deck's wood short and sharp.

"What do we do now?" asked Teague.

The question rattled around in Kyle's head with all of the other thoughts and emotions she had been dealing with. She was overwhelmed by the anxiety of not knowing. She could think of nothing just then to get them all to safety, and the more she tried, the more agitated she became. With a long sigh, she said the only thing that felt like it made sense. "We sleep."

She could only hope everything would be better in the morning.

6.

The next day was not better.

Nor the next one.

Nor the next.

As the days aboard the ship that had formerly belonged to only her stretched on, Kyle found herself forced into the role of navigator. Apparently, in Vána's infinite wisdom, she had not thought to bring a navigator worth their salt. There was no one among those she brought that was more than passably good at navigation. Better astronomers than anything, they found their way best at night than in the cloudless azure skies of the daytime.

"But you have the sun and the tools you need," Kyle insisted. "There's no necessity for me to steer and navigate."

The Adalarian woman glared at Kyle. "Vána has ordered that you helm *The Stargazer* by day and so it shall be. My limitations are academic." Without a second glance, she turned and walked away, leaving Kyle to wonder just how much of this excursion had been planned out before Vána started out with her loyal soldiers. One would think to find more intention and knowledge on a journey to find the Well of Eternal Life.

So, despite her protestations, Kyle was conscripted and forced to the helm. And forced she had to be. The only force that had finally gotten her moving were the veiled threats that Vána had made against Kyle's loved ones. Had it only been Kyle, she might have stubbornly refused despite all talk and adamantly gotten herself killed, or at least seriously injured, by her progenitor.

Not only was she required to guide the ship across the waters, but in being pressed into the task, she was separated from Teague, and it stung. At the end of the day, she returned to their shared quarters, but it was usually with exhaustion so deep that she could do little but offer a kiss and wish of a good night before dropping into slumber. She missed Teague to a point that made her heart ache.

Teague was likewise put to work. Their place was to aid in the preparation of meals for Vána and her crew. Teague knew a number of Adalarian dishes thanks to living and working so much in the cultural amalgam that was the Saltskiff Bazaar. A diverse menu meant a larger population of customers, and so they had worked on expanding their culinary skills beyond the common offerings one might find in a port inn. Because of this, Teague went so far as to impress many of Vána's followers with their cooking and gained more than one nod of approval. They even collected one or two compliments, spoken *aloud*.

Kyle couldn't blame the soldiers, either. The savory, spiced smells that wafted from the galley were mouth-watering. Apparently, the old adage—the way to one's heart was through their stomach—held some truth to it. At least one of the two of them was making allies. Well, perhaps not allies, but less ardent enemies. It was something.

Kyle was having far less success in winning anyone over from Vána's camp. On her first day at the helm, she talked herself hoarse trying to convince Vána, Valeria, or any of the guards that what they were doing was an incredibly poor life choice. Mentions of the deadly tales of the storms or the fact that no one had ever returned from an excursion from the Elysium Cove, fell on heedless ears. The rewards for her trouble were cold stares, and at the end of the day, a nasty bruise along her cheekbone, compliments of Vána's fist. Vána followed the assault up with more of her vicious threats against Teague, Phaiden, and Nico, just to drive her point deeper.

Quite frankly, the menacing was getting old.

Nevertheless, from that point onward Kyle kept her mouth shut. She spoke only when directly ordered to. Unfortunately for Vána, this had an unintended but decidedly deleterious effect on her recruits. They were not very skilled shipmen, and their lack of knowledge showed in more than one dangerous accident. One poor man was dragged up the main mast by a rope he had inadvertently looped around his arm. Another of the guards was nearly crushed when they untied the lashing that kept a cannon anchored and it had pinned them to the deck railing. Kyle, for her part, had no intention of saving them from themselves.

If she had only been able to keep from chuckling after one fell from the rigging, she might have spared herself the grief of dealing with Vána again.

"Your sailors could use more schooling," Kyle murmured when Vána confronted her.

"You little...you knew he would fall. You know when they're doing something dangerous," she hissed, then struck Kyle hard enough to split her lip.

"I'm only following orders," Kyle snapped back, wiping at the blood that dripped from the cut. "I was told to remain silent, so I did. It isn't my fault that your followers are incompetent deckhands. At this rate, they'll all be dead before we even set eyes on the Elysium Cove storms."

Vána's jaw tightened with such severity that Kyle thought it might snap. She swore she could hear the woman's teeth grinding. Kyle wanted to retort, but she knew it would be unwise to do so. Vána's rigid back and the bulging, throbbing vein in her forehead told Kyle that she was one comment away from unhinging the Adalarian leader. The reply wasn't worth the risk, so she held her tongue instead and watched as Vána cast her one last long, warning glare before stomping away.

From then on, Kyle was on her best behavior. If it meant not being a smart ass, then that was what she would have to do. Outwardly, anyway.

Besides, her energy needed to be pushed towards attempting to get everyone on the ship out of the mess Vána was intent on forcing them into. Still, as days slipped by and Kyle searched for some weakness she could use, nothing she plotted was enough to overcome the advantage of numbers that the Adalarians had over her. For a brief time, at least, she clung to the hope that what Valeria had said was true and that she was working to convince Vána that this was all a mistake. Even then, Kyle had difficulty finding the time to speak to her aunt. It wasn't until the evening of the eighth day that an opportunity to sneak in a conversation finally presented itself.

The sun was setting, glittering like dying fire against the darkening surface of the water. Despite it being summer, the day had been unseasonably cool, and Kyle felt the exhaustion both from being at the helm since dawn and from shivering throughout much of that time. Her hands were painfully stiff, and her legs ached from the rocking in place she had been doing to keep the blood flowing. The day's workers were heading below decks and the night watch was coming to replace them. Kyle was relieved to see her own replacement coming to supplant her at her forced post. Thank the depths for small favors.

As casually as she could, Kyle strolled over to Valeria. She was trying to look inconspicuous, as if her moving to speak to Vána's second-in-command was as normal as anything else aboard the ship. Given how close Valeria stood to the door for the Captain's quarters—the ones Vána had stolen and now called her own—Kyle had no desire to be seen as a threat.

"Valeria," she hissed, attempting to get her aunt's attention and no one else's. "Have you made any progress with your ma?"

Valeria did not move to look at her and kept her expression mild as she straightened up. "I have had many a conversation and am working on convincing her that she would be better off abandoning this journey," she murmured, finally. "Mother can be headstrong, especially when it comes to her loyalty to the Courts of Adalar."

Loyalty? Kyle fought not to laugh. Instead, she said, "Given she's disobeying a direct order, I can only assume that's a joke. I didn't know you knew how to joke."

"They never ordered her not to go," Valeria insisted, and her voice sharpened defensively. "They simply informed her that they would not supply the ships needed for the voyage."

"Ah, yes. Let's split hairs as the woman leads us all to certain death." Kyle couldn't keep the sardonic edge from her words. "Loyalty, indeed."

It was then that Valeria turned to her, fire in her eyes. "You have no right to judge her. You do not have the vaguest inkling of what she has been through," she snapped. Her voice was earnest, nearly pleading. It was plain that Valeria was seeking understanding and empathy from her niece.

Kyle didn't care. She would give neither. "Whatever she has or has not been through does not give her the right to do all of this. She insists on leading good people to their doom in this spectacle of horrific decision-making. By the depths, Valeria, if not by her words and actions, what am I supposed to judge her on?"

Valeria's eyes narrowed and something deep within Kyle squeezed painfully. Maybe it was the last shreds of hope of some connection to her mother's family, but it stung as she watched disappointment wash over her aunt's face. Perhaps Valeria had been hoping to find a sympathetic ear in her niece, but she had been completely disillusioned with that idea. Her features shifted from hurt to a cold, stern mask that completely shut Kyle out.

"Guard," Valeria snapped, voice low. Now her gaze was pinned to Kyle, eyes hard. "The former captain needs to be escorted to the evening meal."

Kyle forced a placid smile. She was conflicted. She had meant to gain her aunt's support, but she could not say she was sorry that Valeria had reacted this way. After all, her mother's family had never had much care or concern for Kyle after her mother died. They had barely shown any before her death, either. Why should Kyle trust them, *any* of them, to do right by her?

The guard stepped up beside Kyle, but Valeria raised a hand to stop him, giving Kyle room to speak.

In as untroubled a tone as she could manage, Kyle said, "I need no escort. I know perfectly well how to find my way in my own ship. I am also familiar with the consequences the Raudnost family will visit on me if I don't *behave,* so there is no worry of a fight. They have proven time and time again that they have no qualms hurting the innocent for their own gain."

Valeria flinched, the barb hitting deep, but Kyle didn't stay to relish whatever small victory it might have been. She compelled herself into a saunter towards the stairs, maintaining her unbothered air as she hurried down the steps and onto the gun deck. She kept her head down, ignoring any of Vána's people as she strode across the gun deck to take the second set of stairs down to the orlop deck. Instead of going to the galley, however, she moved to the infirmary. She breezed past the guard at the door and into the sick room with indifference, shutting it behind her.

One of the few "*freedoms*" she had been afforded for the duration of the journey was to be permitted a sliver of privacy when visiting her father and brother in the infirmary. The guard beyond the door was no doubt trying to listen, but the door was thick, good wood and would only give away raised voices. She would take her victories where she could get them.

Ioan sat at the small desk. A pair of spectacles were perched on his nose as he measured liquid from a darkened bottle into a small cup using a glass vial. He was intent on his task but spared her a sideways glance when she entered and closed the door.

"How are your charges today?" Kyle asked him, running a hand through her short, dark hair and letting out a long sigh. It didn't offer much, but the infirmary was a place she felt she could let down her constant vigilance.

She could see for herself that Nico lay with his blanket pulled up to his shoulders. He still looked pale, but not as poorly as he had earlier in the week, and he was asleep propped more on his good side, the pillows from the other cots helping to keep him in a position so as not to exacerbate any wounds.

Phaiden, on the other hand, was seated on his cot. A deck of playing cards had been laid out in front of him and he seemed to be making a game of matching the suits. The cut on his forehead was healing nicely and covered by just a bit of bandage and poultice. His leg jutted out and over the edge of the cot, the splint that Ioan had insisted on holding the limb at an awkward angle. The Adalarian healer had suspected a break and wanted to make sure it would be kept from too much jostling. Phaiden's other leg was on the bed, a shackle encircling the ankle and a chain running beneath the bed and affixed to the cot. It was something Vána had insisted on. One more thing to hold against the Adalarian elder. Just looking at it stoked Kyle's anger.

Noticing her growing irritation, Phaiden offered his secondborn a winning grin. "I was never much of a favorite in Vána's eyes." He thought for a moment, then added, "She isn't a very good mother-in-law."

"That's because she isn't one, at least not to you. You never married Ma," was Kyle's retort.

"Nuance."

Ioan spoke up before Phaiden could say anything more. "Your father has repeatedly ignored almost every recommendation I give him. When I ask him to rest, he feels the need to be hopping around the room. Well... as far as his tether will allow him, anyway. When I want him up so I can examine the leg, he becomes an immovable object." Finishing his task, Ioan put a stopper in the dark bottle and put it securely on the shelf, before moving to offer Phaiden the small cup he had been measuring liquid into. "Here, drink this. It will help with the swelling."

Phaiden made a face but accepted the cup and rifled down the contents.

"That does sound like him," Kyle replied, watching him hand the cup back to Ioan. "Normally, his willfulness is endearing, but under the current circumstances..." She trailed off.

"It is less so," Ioan offered.

"Yes."

"I can't help it. I'm a free spirit," Phaiden said. He leaned back on the cot, putting his hands behind his head and grinning. "Where do you think you and your brother get it?"

Kyle knew he was seeking compliments and refused to give them to him. Instead, she offered another question to Ioan. "And Nico? How is he?"

"He has been in and out of slumber. I think the danger of infection has mostly passed. He insists the pain from his injuries is tolerable, but I can see how the man tenses and flinches at the lightest touch. He is simply trying to push through the discomfort, which does little to aid healing," Ioan explained quietly. He put the cup back among the infirmary's accouterments and let out a long breath. "I gave him something to ease the pain and help him sleep. I'm hoping that deeper rest will mean he is back on his feet sooner."

"Is that why he's still asleep?" Kyle's voice sounded small, even to herself.

"Partly. The other part is that he lost a lot of blood. While his wounds will heal, he will be exhausted for quite some time."

"And we can do nothing to help?" asked Phaiden. His boyish smile had faded a bit, and there was concern etched into the worried lines on his face.

Ioan grunted. "There are certain foods, ones that are good for the blood, that we could give him that would help, but it would still be a slow process." He tossed a glare at the closed door. "Even if they were available, I doubt her *highness* and her mindless followers would allow them to us." He looked from Kyle to Phaiden and appeared to realize that while his anger towards his leader was appreciated, it wasn't very reassuring. He huffed. "I will look out as best I can for him."

Phaiden nodded. "Ioan here has already been good about getting as much as he can from them, and you know how much of a pain in the ass I can be." While only a half jest, his voice was still jovial and heartening.

He reached a hand out and on reflex Kyle did the same. There was a moment of relief when she felt the familiar, calloused hand of her father give her own a reassuring squeeze. She might not ever admit it, but having her father there was one of the only things keeping her grounded in this whole mess. Countless memories tumbled together of times Phaiden had been there to keep her company in storms or chase away the nightmares of a much younger self. Having someone she trusted as deeply as Phaiden at her back, and to protect Nico, kept much of her fear from overwhelming her. She couldn't imagine pushing through this crisis without him.

"Is there a plan yet?" Phaiden asked.

The question jarred Kyle out of her thoughts. She hesitated, then finally admitted it. "No. Valeria is avoiding any direct conflict with her mother. She will offer us no help."

Ioan cursed softly to himself.

Phaiden nodded. "We may have..." he trailed off, studying his daughter's hand in his. Clearing his throat, he began again. "We may have to use the storm to our advantage."

"That puts us uncomfortably close to the Elysium Cove, does it not?" asked Ioan. "Are we really in such dire straits?"

"We may have no choice," Phaiden pressed.

Kyle hadn't wanted to consider the possibility and had been dreading her father bringing it up. She knew he would, sooner or later. "He's right," she said and heaved a heavy sigh.

"By Adal," murmured Ioan. "What does that mean for us?"

"Wresting control from Vána during the storm would be our best bet," Phaiden suggested. "When we are still far from serious danger, mind you."

"Easy for you to say when you are chained to the infirmary," Kyle whined.

"Do you really think this flimsy thing can hold me?" Phaiden asked, poking at the chain. "Please, child. Give me more credit than that."

Kyle couldn't stop the smile that crept over her face. "All right, all right. We will speak more of this, but not now. Valeria is angry at me, and I should go before she has me dragged out by my hair." She cast one last look at her sleeping brother, then to Ioan and Phaiden. "Stay safe. We'll figure something out."

7.

The orlop deck was dark, the bustling sounds and sweet, savory smells of the evening meal having faded. They gave way to the warm wood scent of the ship and the soft hint of saltwater that hung eternally in the air no matter where one was on *The Stargazer*.

One lantern, turned low, hung at the far end of the carpentry storage room where Kyle and Teague were now forced to sleep. A single guard was stationed just beyond the open doorway. Even in the low light, Kyle could see the woman, standing erect, eyes forward. She was turned away, but Kyle was sure that she would be listening for any sign of rebellion.

As if any sort of insurrection was a possibility. No, Kyle had been forced to resign herself to biding her time. Discussions had occurred, and a tentative plan was put in place in the day or so since Kyle had argued with Valeria, but there was nothing that could be done yet. As much as she wanted to swing into action and save the day like the dashing hero she wished she was, some acts of heroism would have to wait.

She lay in her hammock, eyes fixed on the wood of the far wall, watching the lantern's glow move with every bob and sway of the waves on which *The Stargazer* rode.

It was a difficult thing, to be so humbled. To see her family be so degraded. After all, her brother was a captain in Sursum's navy. Wasn't he meant to be trained in fighting off the enemy? And seeing her father, *the* Phaiden Talos, being anything but a victor in a struggle he found himself in, strained the bounds of her imagination. Despite having grown up into her own woman, some part of Kyle still saw him as a giant. The man was a hero. He had made enemies, surely, but the list of friends he boasted meant he should have been safe from this sort of thing. It should not have happened to either of them and yet—

A whisper interrupted her thoughts.

The hammock above her rocked gently, and Kyle could make out the shape of Teague peeking over the edge, large eyes showing endless depths in the warm half-light of the lantern. They pointed down to Kyle with one graceful hand and Kyle instantly knew what they were asking. She nodded her agreement, inviting Teague to join her. They did not need further encouragement and slipped out of their hammock and into Kyle's.

The guard in the hall shifted and Kyle glared, defiant. Vána could choose the direction of the ship, among many things, but Kyle would be damned before she allowed her or her guards to dictate whether Kyle was allowed to cuddle with the person that she loved.

Teague, meanwhile, curled up into Kyle's side, making themself small despite their greater height. They laid their head on the young captain's shoulder and sighed. The only sounds around them were the gentle creak of the ship and the muffled tread of Vána's followers on the gun deck above.

Teague spoke in a barely audible whisper. "I wonder if it would have been wiser to have stayed in my room back on Saltskiff," they murmured, a smile in their voice. "Might have saved us both the trouble."

Kyle knew it was meant to be a light jest, but she stiffened all the same, anger and anxiety gripping at her insides with equal fervor. If she'd had even the smallest inkling as to what had been waiting for her at *The Stargazer*, Kyle would never have brought Teague with her. She had spent so much time since then cursing her own bad luck. She could not help but wonder if it would be better if, once they all managed to slip out of this whole mess, she and Teague parted ways. After all, this life was not without its dangers. Was it fair to ask anyone to make the choice between a safer, quieter life, and the apparent possibility of kidnap and conscription into a fool's errand that could kill them all? Teague would be better off without her.

The mere thought squeezed the air from Kyle's lungs. Unconsciously, her arm tightened around Teague's shoulders, seeking the comfort her thoughts were taking from her.

It didn't help. She couldn't quiet her thoughts, and each repetition of *Teague would be better off without her* cut a new, raw hole in her heart. Embracing her love was doing very little to assuage that violence.

The lantern's light was nearly spent, and in the steadily growing darkness, the ship rocked around them. Kyle Talos had no witticisms that could save the day. She couldn't even bring herself out of her own mental spiral. In the steadily growing darkness, she felt smaller and smaller with each passing moment.

Tears stung the back of her eyes and she inhaled sharply, fighting the sob that was slowly climbing up her throat.

It was then that Teague shifted, sliding an arm over and around Kyle's waist and pulling her closer while nuzzling their head against her throat. They placed a small kiss on her neck and Kyle shivered, relaxing ever so slightly.

"I don't know if this is the time," Kyle murmured as she breathed a shaky laugh. She was relieved to hear that she sounded amused rather than ready to fall to pieces.

Teague chuckled. Their lips were so close to Kyle's skin that she could feel their breath. "True. Hopefully soon. Perhaps once this is all over and we are back, you can find a way to propose then? Without all of this 'being abducted by your estranged grandmother' nonsense?"

Kyle nodded in the darkness, then started as the meaning of her lover's words sank in. Teague had known? Shifting to glance down into their face, she asked, "Wait, what? How did you know?"

A giggle was their only response for a moment. Then they finally managed, "Bess is horrible with keeping secrets."

Bess had betrayed Kyle? She had sworn the eldest Dailann sibling to secrecy when she'd asked for help arranging the evening. For some reason, Kyle had thought that her eagerness to help and offer to accommodate the event had equated to her keeping quiet about it as well. Kyle relaxed her grip around Teague's shoulder, pulling back just enough to look at Teague. "I trusted her!" she shrilled.

"Ky, the poor woman tells Arthur and me *everything*. She has never met a secret she did not share."

There was a pause, then they both laughed.

Kyle heard the guard shifting just beyond the doorway. They didn't enter, though.

"Is that why you came with me? Because you knew?"

"Perhaps," Teague offered, with a grin. The playful smile faded quickly, and Teague moved her head back to Kyle's shoulder, snuggling against her. "Well, that and I wanted to make sure you would be safe." They thought for a moment before continuing. "You need someone to have your back, should anything happen."

"And clearly something has."

"True. I have to admit, I didn't think all of this would occur." Teague shook their head and let out a sigh. Their arm tightened, pulling Kyle's body closer to their own. "But I am here for you, dangerous adventure or no."

Kyle stilled. Teague's words were sending shivers through her entire being. "Does that mean..." she trailed off, nerves wavering. She didn't dare assume. There was too much unknown. But what if these were the only moments they might have left together? Soon they would reach the cove, and the uncertainty of what could happen clawed at her. No one had ever braved the storms and lived to tell the tale. What proof was there that they could be the first? None. That meant that every moment, every second mattered so much more.

Her resolve strengthened and she forced herself to speak. "Does that mean you would be willing to always accompany me? To be with me, as my spouse?"

"Of course," was the reply, without a moment's hesitation. "Though once this is all over, I am still holding you to a wonderfully romantic breakfast, an elaborate proposal, and lovemaking that lasts for hours afterwards." They gave another little squeeze to Kyle before letting out a yawn.

In half an instant, Kyle went from anxiety to elation. It was a startling change. To be so flooded with joy, all at once, was nearly overwhelming. Before she could do anything to express it, her mind caught on a handful of Teague's words.

Once this is all over.

Would any of them find themselves alive on the other side of this when it was? Or were they destined to be debris along the battered shores of the Elysium Cove?

"Love," Kyle began, voice thick. "I'm not sure, if—"

Teague interrupted, their voice firm and tone final. "There *will* be an after for us, Kyle Talos. Somehow. Someway." They shifted again, this time getting into a more comfortable position. The weight of their arm across Kyle's waist offered comfort and reassurance. "We will make sure of it."

Kyle relented, allowing herself to believe Teague's words instead of the doubting voice at the back of her mind. The severity of her thoughts had abated, chased away by the accepted proposal of marriage. She wouldn't celebrate yet, though. She would save it for after. Once they were safe and sailing off into the sunset.

Kyle shifted a bit so that Teague's head rested in the hollow of her shoulder and so she could rest her cheek on Teague's golden hair. She placed a gentle kiss on Teague's head and let her eyes drift shut, thinking of better times.

The two lovers fell asleep, gently cradled in the safety of *The Stargazer*.

8.

Dawn had yet to break day on the fading night, but dread already weighed heavily in Kyle's chest. The significance of what was coming dragged on her, and every movement she made was forced. She rose and dressed quickly, moving quietly in the heavy darkness. When she was done, she looked to Teague, who slept peacefully in their hammock. After worrying she might wake them, she took the risk and placed a kiss on Teague's forehead.

"What? Is it something?" Teague asked. Their voice was slurred and thick with sleep, and it brought a smile to Kyle's face.

"Sleep while you have time, love," Kyle whispered. Her voice still cracked on the words, buckling under the heft of the fear behind them, but Teague was too sleep-addled to notice. They mumbled their thanks and love before drifting back to sleep.

Kyle watched them for a long moment, steeling herself for the coming day. If her calculations were correct, they would reach the Elysium Cove today.

The knowledge buzzed, unpleasant and insistent, at the back of Kyle's mind as she left the confines of the carpentry storage. The more she thought about it, the harder her heart pounded, and the tips of her fingers tingled with either anticipation or anxiety. She couldn't tell which.

Moving past the spot in the hallway where a guard had been posted, she noticed with small satisfaction that it was deserted. A good sign. It meant that the plan was already working.

Her first stop was the infirmary.

The man who had been standing stalwart guard the night before now lay slumped, half-seated on the floor. His head was tilted back, a light

59

snore escaped his gaping mouth and drool trickled down from the corner of his lips. His lantern was on the floor beside him, the glow stifled by its closed shutters. She took it, opening the slats and turning up the flame ever so slightly. The guard didn't stir as she gently relieved him off his sidearm, an expensive short sword of Adalarian quality. Stepping quietly around him, she gingerly opened the door to the infirmary and stepped inside, closing herself in.

In the warm glow from the lantern, Kyle saw that Nico slept peacefully in his cot and Ioan did the same on a cot at the farthest end of the infirmary. The calming aroma of lavender and mint did little to assuage her nerves, and part of her wished that Ioan was awake to mix something to quiet her pounding heart. Only Phaiden was awake, sitting like a gargoyle on the edge of his cot. He winced as she entered and gestured for her to turn down the light.

"Are you ready?" he asked, his voice the barest whisper. "I can feel the waters growing rougher."

"Did it wake you as well?" Kyle asked, voice taut. As soon as she asked it, she knew it was a foolish question. Phaiden Talos had lived and breathed the seas since he was fourteen and had stowed away on his first boat. He knew the seas better than he knew himself. The sensations of *The Stargazer* entering rougher waters had woken her. She could only imagine how much earlier he had been alerted to it.

He nodded. "The plan?"

Kyle took a moment, recalling everything they had discussed in the last handful of days. "Aggressive persuasion. I try to talk Vána and her followers out of this ridiculous quest one final time. If it doesn't work, I give the order to furl the rear sails and that will be the signal for you and Ioan to come to my aid. We'll do our best to take over the ship and get the hell out of here." She held the sword she had taken from the guard out to her father. Phaiden accepted it without comment, tucking it out of sight beneath his cot.

"And Teague did their part?" he asked after hiding the weapon.

It was Kyle's turn to nod. "Yes. They put enough solanacia milk in the meal last night that half of Vána's forces will sleep through most of the day and into the evening. Even the guard at your door was fast asleep."

"Good. All we will have to deal with are those on deck. Hopefully, they will be exhausted from working throughout the night."

Kyle fidgeted in the lantern light. She hated how nervous she felt, as if this was her first time in a dangerous situation. They had a plan, and she could count on her father to execute it. After all, much of it was his own plot. Even still, she found that the added weight of responsibility for her brother and Teague, even to some extent Phaiden and even Ioan, put her on edge.

"I wish I had *my* weapons." It would be a comfort to have arms she was familiar with by her side. In taking over her quarters, Vána had cut Kyle off from her sword and parrying dagger. She flexed her hands, missing their weight and reassurance.

"Even if we could get to them, we cannot risk tipping Vána off that we have something planned. We can manage without." Phaiden stood and wrapped Kyle in a tight hug. "You're a Talos. You'll make it work."

Kyle allowed herself a moment to rest her forehead on his shoulder. Her heart slowed and she felt herself relax, if only by a sliver. Distantly, she realized he was already free of the shackle that had been around his ankle last time she had seen him. He had probably only been wearing the damned thing for the sake of appearances. She grinned. "Time to show Ma's side of the family what we are capable of."

"That's my kiddo." He took a step back and ruffled her hair. "Besides, your mother never had a complaint about what I could do." He gave her a winning, roguish grin.

"That's disgusting, Da."

Chuckling, Phaiden nodded towards the door. "Now get out there. I'll be rousing Ioan and we will be waiting for the signal."

Kyle emerged from the infirmary as silently as she had entered it. She eyed the sleeping guard for a moment before she bent down and took hold of his ankles. As quietly as she could manage, she dragged him across the deck, bringing the unconscious man to the area normally used for any livestock that might be on board. Since there was none, she thought it would be a safe, out-of-the-way spot to stow him. She tucked him in a corner and half-covered him with what bits of hay and straw she could find. "Sleep tight," she murmured.

She returned for the lantern and made her way up the stairs to the gun deck. She tread quickly and quietly past the rows of silent guns. Two guards lay sleeping here as well, and Kyle did her best to hide them in the shadows of the cannons. In the haze of the predawn, she hoped they would go unnoticed. When she was done, she went up the next set of stairs and onto the main deck.

When Kyle stepped out from within the depths of *The Stargazer* she was greeted with a sky brimming with thick, dark clouds. The sun wouldn't be able to break through their bulk and so had settled for casting gray, silvery light on the distant horizon. The dense pall from the skies made everything murky and ominous, and a thin mist of drizzle fell over the ship. Sharp winds gusted, pulling at the sails above and making them snap and dance with its force.

In the distance—not far enough for Kyle's comfort—she could see what looked to be a swirling, churning mass of clouds, lightning, and roiling waves. Thunder rumbled angrily around them. There was no denying what she was seeing. Beyond a shadow of a doubt, she knew that they were within sight of the tempest that surrounded the Elysium Cove.

Every child knew the tales of the Well of Eternal Life and the Elysium Cove. It had been one of Kyle's favorite bedtime stories when she had been only knee-high. Legends told that the world was once only sand and heat until one day, the well overflowed, bringing the waters to the world. It filled the oceans and the seas, and what was left was thought to bestow the gift of immortality on anyone brave enough to venture to it. The storm was there to protect the well. Who had put the storm there? A god? A powerful sorcerer? There was more than one story, and Kyle thought all of them were complete fiction. Oh, the storm existed, but eternal life? That was the stuff of fairy tales.

The dread she had been feeling since waking settled cold and painful in her gut as she strode towards the helm.

The Adalarian guard who had been steering the ship throughout the night wore her stress and exhaustion plainly on her pale face, the delicate skin beneath her eyes darkened by the lack of sleep. When Kyle approached, the guard gave her a look of worry, glancing between Vána at her side and Kyle. It seemed that at least this follower was less confident in Vána than she had been when the sun set the day before. She also looked pale, almost green. Rougher waters tended to roil the stomach. Kyle wondered how many of the Adalarian followers would suffer trials of faith and fortitude when confronted with the reality of the storm they were attempting to fight.

"You are relieved of your post," Vána cooly said to the Adalarian woman. The guard did not need to be told twice. She hurried off, head bowed.

Vána watched her go, then turned her icy gaze to her grandchild, a smug expression on her face. Around her neck, the pendant glowed a soft blue color, its gleam throbbing as if rejoicing at how close it was to the shores of the Elysium Cove. "I am so glad that it will be you, Kalina, leading us into this glorious triumph. You will see with your own eyes how wrong your doubts were."

"It's Kyle, not Kalina," Kyle muttered under her breath, but the words were covered by a sudden gust of watery wind. She took hold of the ship's wheel, moving to stand just a bit in front and to the left of Vána. Looking out over the horizon, Kyle immediately caught sight of the storm again. She took a deep breath, remembering the conversation with her father.

All she could do was try.

"Vána, this won't work. You are sailing all of us, yourself included, into certain death," she began. She didn't dare look back at the older woman, instead staring straight ahead. "The winds themselves will tear the ship apart before we are close enough to—"

"Silence," Vána snapped, interrupting Kyle's plea. She leaned forward, her head next to Kyle's, her chin nearly resting on her shoulder. "And in case you have any thoughts of attempting to sabotage this endeavor." She gave a short, sharp nod towards one of her followers, and the follower shouted below decks.

Kyle felt her heart sink as Teague and Phaiden were led up to the main deck. Her father was now shackled hand and foot, and while Teague was left unbound, the grip the guard had on their arm looked tight and painful. When Phaiden raised his head to meet his daughter's gaze, she saw one of his eyes was swollen and bruising. He gave a barely perceptible shake of his head, but it told Kyle all. Any semblance of the plan they had formed had failed almost before it started.

Vána continued, her words turning Kyle's blood to ice.

"The guards I've had posted outside the infirmary have *excellent* hearing. They did not know of the solanacia, I have to admit, but it is no matter. We can still continue the voyage with those that are awake. You have not destroyed our chances for success." She chortled, softly. "But do anything else and I will personally throw your loved ones overboard."

Involuntarily, Kyle took a step towards them, but Vána stretched out a hand, grabbing her shoulder in a tight grip that made the younger woman gasp in pain. "Now child, you *will* sail us towards the storm."

Kyle had no other choice and did as she was commanded.

Within little more than an hour, what began as a light drizzle and choppy waters had become a tempest. The waves had risen dangerously, slamming into the hull again and again. Winds ripped at the sails and rain drove on the backs of the violent gusts.

Vána's guards were coping as best they could, but it was obvious none of them had much experience at sea. Some kept the faith, working with dogged determination. Others were less sanguine at the odds of the journey meeting success. Fear drained the color from their faces, and they clutched desperately to the railing, rigging, mast, or whatever else they felt was secured fast to the deck.

Kyle wasn't used to sailing in such a storm, especially without a full and knowledgeable crew. She had never encountered rough waters of this magnitude. She would have given anything for her crew to have her back now. "Rig lifelines, fore and aft," she shouted as the boat pitched from a wave.

"What?" asked a guard. "What does that—"

"The ropes," Kyle ordered. "Run them from the front of the boat to the back and fasten them well. Use them as guides. Hold onto them for safety when moving along the deck!"

"Here," came another shout. Valeria was there, holding coils of rope. She handed one to the guard, directing him on where and how to affix them even as she tied the other ends. Once the lines were tied, she returned to Kyle, her yell barely audible above the sound of crashing waves and rolling thunder. "What do you need next?"

"The sails," Kyle called, projecting her voice as much as possible to be heard over the storm. "The wind is going to destroy them. Furl the sails at the aft first, to keep the ship from being pushed sideways."

Valeria nodded and rushed off with two of Vána's followers to see the task done.

Amid the uproar, Vána remained impassive, her stoic form rigid and unyielding despite the squall rioting around them.

Kyle was currently sailing around the southern point of the Elysium Cove. Vána insisted the best point of entry would be there, and the direction suited Kyle just as well as any. She knew, at least for the time being, sailing into the storm at an angle meant the bow of the ship—the strongest part of her—was what would take the brunt of the storm, slicing through it with relative ease. Of course, she also knew that it wouldn't do any of them any good if they got too close to shore in conditions like this. It would destroy the bottom of the boat and leave them stranded at the mercy of the apocalyptic tempest.

Kyle guided the ship as well as she could in the tossing waves, the helm fighting her for each and every league she managed. Everything ached. Trying to keep her footing on wet wood, as the boat rocked, the wind howled, the rain drove, and the ship's wheel pulled, was wearing her to the very bone. Her hands were raw, and she felt blisters forming, but she had no choice.

Worst of all, she knew that they hadn't hit the most powerful part of the storm yet.

Vána, however, was unperturbed. The closer *The Stargazer* got to the supposed entry to the cove, the more distant the woman's gaze became. She was steadily vanishing into her own thoughts of triumph and glory.

Is this my chance? Kyle wondered. Was this the flaw in Vána's armor that Kyle had been waiting for? Unsure, she hesitated.

"Vána!" came a cry. It was Valeria. She held tightly to the lifeline that had been tied and used it to guide her while she moved. "It is too dangerous. We need to turn back to keep everyone safe!"

"No!" Vána shouted though she was barely paying attention to her daughter. Her cold eyes were scanning the storm, looking for a way in. "This is more important!"

"More important than our lives?"

"*I will have this,*" Vána volleyed back.

Valeria shook her head and moved up the deck, stopping at the guard who had a hold of Phaiden. She gave the follower an order that Kyle couldn't hear. The guard nodded, his expression relieved, and hauled Phaiden to his feet and towards the stairs. The two of them banished into the ship, and Kyle could breathe at least a small sigh of relief at knowing her father was no longer in danger of falling overboard.

Now it was far more likely he would simply drown like the rest of them when the boat sank.

"There!" Vána screamed, pointing off to the port side.

Kyle squinted to see through the storm. With the wind and rain, she couldn't glean much. In fact, she saw no break in the tempest. She looked to Vána, then back to the tourbillon, but there was nothing but chaos in the roiling ocean, swirling clouds, and falling rain. The truth was harsh and unforgiving. There was no break. If Vána saw one, it was one her mind wanted her to see, and Kyle knew that Vána would force her to sail into the maelstrom.

You are steering a ship of death.

Some distant, rosy part of her had hoped that Vána had been right. That the silly glowing crystal would lead them safely through the storm. Now, seeing that there was no truth to it, she knew the only reality was one of fatality. The realization hit her with such force that it knocked the breath from her lungs. She was staring at her end. At everyone's end. It froze her. She was terrified and her white-knuckle grip on the helm meant she wasn't correcting course to follow Vána's guidance.

Vána noticed immediately.

"Damn you, child. Steer to port or we will miss it!" Vána practically roared.

Kyle blinked, temporarily freed from her paralysis. Instead of paying Vána any heed, she looked to Teague.

Teague, who was still on deck. They, along with their guard, were hanging to the ropes for dear life. Despite the danger, Teague was looking up to her. Their eyes met Kyle's across the storm. Desperation and pleading were in Kyle's heart as she tried to convey all of her doubts and fears.

This is the end if we don't do something.

Teague offered Kyle a calm smile, encouraging and warm. Then they wrapped their arm around the lifeline, bracing themselves before giving Kyle a determined nod.

Kyle returned the gesture and took a deep breath, knowing what came next. With every bit of strength she had left, she turned *The Stargazer* hard to starboard.

The ship pitched violently in response to the sudden change in direction. Unprepared for the upheaval, Vána let out a scream and fell into the wheel, her weight helping Kyle keep the ship on its new course. *The Stargazer* was headed away from the Elysium Cove, from the fabled Well of Eternal Life, and from her grandmother's great ambition.

The guard that had been holding Teague's arm fell against the railing, releasing his prisoner in favor of saving himself. Teague quickly used the rope as a guide, pulling themselves towards the steps to the lower deck.

Good. They're safe. Kyle was relieved.

"You *bitch*," Vána screamed, righting herself. She snatched at Kyle, who dodged away from the grasp, still holding the helm as best she could. Vána didn't have a physical weapon, but Kyle knew this made her no less deadly. It just put them on an even footing.

Then Kyle saw the older woman's lips moving, and her hands glowed with an angry, crimson light.

Magic. Vána knew magic. How could Kyle forget?

So much for being on even footing.

Vána reached for Kyle and the ship's captain could hear the hiss of rain turning to steam when it touched Vána's hands. She dodged again, still holding the wheel, but knowing there would not be many more opportunities to avoid her grandmother's enchanted touch. She could feel the heat from the red glow each time she managed to avoid contact.

The older woman grabbed for Kyle's wrist, and Kyle was forced to make the split-second decision of letting go of the helm or suffering the consequences.

Unwilling to give up control of her ship, she would suffer.

Searing hot pain shot up Kyle's arm when Vána's hand wrapped around the exposed wrist, burning her viciously. Involuntarily, Kyle tried to pull away. She released the helm and the wheel spun wildly as the rudder was dragged by the tossing waves below. The ship pitched again, this time struck by a swell of ocean water that hammered the hull. It splashed up and over the deck, spraying them all with the roiling, foaming seas. Kyle lost her footing, falling back and sliding across the slick wood. She raked her hands across the deck as she did, blindly grabbing for the rope but not finding it. Instead, she hit the railing *hard*.

She curled on her side. The skin on her wrist and forearm was charred from the heat of Vána's fiery touch and had begun to peel, the flesh beneath the ruined skin blistered and red. The rain and wind around her made it hard to hear anything but the storm and the pain made it impossible to catch her reeling thoughts. She didn't notice Vána come up on her. It wasn't until a rough hand grabbed a handful of her wet hair that she realized she was in real, immediate danger. The hand clutched hard, pulling, and Kyle scrambled to her feet.

"How dare you?" Vána snarled. Her free arm shot out, hand encircling Kyle's throat and squeezing with a strength born of rage.

Kyle had no time to be relieved that the touch didn't burn her. Vána had cut off her breath. She clawed weakly at her, but Vána's grip was absolute. "You stupid little bitch. Do you think you accomplished anything? I'll kill you. I'll kill you and take the ship. It's that simp—"

Suddenly, the pressure on Kyle's throat and hair were gone. She fell to her knees, coughing, finally able to breathe again. She looked up between gasps and saw Teague now struggling with Vána. A new fear filled Kyle with breathtaking speed, and she pushed herself to her feet, moving to try and separate the two of them as they stumbled towards the railing at the stern of the ship.

Finally gaining something resembling an upper hand in the struggle, Teague shoved Vána away hard. The older woman hit the railing but couldn't check her momentum and she pitched overboard, plummeting to the swirling waters below.

Teague staggered, trying to find their footing on the violently rocking ship.

Kyle felt her heart stop.

No, please no. I won't get there in time.

Teague hit the rail awkwardly, and for a moment looked like they might follow Vána, but their clawed grip on the wood kept them from toppling. Instead, they sank safely to the deck, breathing heavily, head in their hands.

Kyle fell beside them, fumbling to check to make sure they weren't injured, sobbing with relief.

"Are you all right?" Teague shouted over the rush of the storm around them.

Kyle's arm stung horribly. Her neck and head throbbed. The storm still raged around them, and they were not remotely out of danger, but in that instant, knowing that Teague was whole and safe was all that mattered, and she nodded vigorously, letting out an almost hysterical laugh. She was so relieved. So damned relieved.

"Captain Talos!"

It was Valeria's voice, thick and choked with emotion, but still audible over the roaring storm around them.

Kyle looked up at her in the driving rain, body tensed in anticipation.

"I saw—" Valeria began, but her voice failed her. She took another breath and shouted. "I saw Elder Raudnost fall from the ship with the last wave, driven by the storm. We should not risk any more lives," she explained, weaving the story that would become truth from this point forward.

Kyle stared, unable to comprehend her aunt's words. It was Teague who nudged her, whispering to her. "I think she's helping."

Looking from Teague to Valeria, Kyle slowly nodded, comprehension dawning.

Valeria blinked rapidly, perhaps to see in the driving rain or maybe to clear tears from her vision. Either way, she asked loudly, "Can you sail us out of this storm and to safety?"

A weight lifted from Kyle's shoulders. At least one of her mother's relations was a halfway decent individual. Not needing a second invitation, Kyle pushed herself to her feet, ignoring the aches and pains that protested the movement. "It would be my pleasure."

9.

The distant, rhythmic sound of knocking pulled Kyle from her sleep. A quiet but insistent drumming that called to her from beyond the depths of her slumber. Remotely she grieved the loss of her repose even as she opened her eyes, wincing at the light that assaulted them.

The sun, barely a sliver on the blessedly clear eastern horizon, shone through the windows of *The Stargazer's* captain's quarters. It took Kyle a moment to realize that she was seeing it because she was back in the captain's quarters, in her own bed, wrapped in her own blankets. She had been restored to being captain of her ship and reclaimed all of the accoutrements that came with it.

Kyle stirred amid the bed coverings, not wanting to give up the warmth of her sanctuary. Sleep had been no easy thing, what with her arm salved, to ease the burns, and bandaged. The pain, while tolerable thanks to Ioan and his apothecary arts, was still present and uncomfortable. Her throat was also bruised and sore, and her body ached all over from the adventures of the previous day. Still, she had managed.

Now her body was refusing to let her sink back into the depths of sleep. With a long and labored sigh, she decided she might as well get up.

Carefully, she stretched. Still half asleep, she reached her uninjured arm over to wrap it around Teague.

Except Teague wasn't there. Kyle found herself embracing nothing.

Suddenly more awake, she pushed herself, glancing fervently around the room in the pale morning light. Nothing. "Teague?" she asked, her voice a small rasp of its usual tone.

Teague poked her head out from just around the corner of the quarters, their long blonde hair swinging around them. They wore a dressing gown which they held closed at the chest to obscure the view of their night shift. Behind them, another face appeared, one that made Kyle grin widely.

"Sorry, did I wake you?" Nico asked. He cocked an eyebrow and shot her a feigned glance of exasperation. "You plan on sleeping the day away, lazybones?"

He looked good but didn't have his usual easy energy. His coloring was still paler than Kyle would have liked to see. Despite the exhaustion that hung on him, he was up and about and that was more than any day since the Saltskiff Bazaar. He was also feeling good enough to jest with her, which she accepted as a good sign of recovery.

"You're one to talk," Kyle croaked, laughing weakly. "You've been asleep this whole trip!"

"With good reason. I nearly died protecting your ship," Nico said, waving a hand dismissively. "Regardless, I am awake now. I was just coming to check on you both." He grinned. "The captain requested that I see that you are all right and that food is brought to you this morning."

It was bait and she knew it, but she took it anyway. "I'm the captain!"

Nico shrugged. "Very well, the *former* captain. Da just wanted me to check on you."

Teague leaned against the warm wood of the cabin, soft light from the windows playing over their blonde tresses. "I think she could use some more rest," they explained, no doubt hiding a smile behind their hand. The amusement faded quickly when their eyes fell on Kyle and the young captain watched as Teague slipped into the role of consummate caretaker. "A hearty meal would not go awry, but in a bit, please. Also, something for the pain?" they continued, moving closer to the bed.

"Ioan said he would come to her once she was awake," Nico assured them.

"Good. Maybe I will stay abed all day," added Kyle in a playful, snotty tone.

Nico rolled his eyes but smiled nevertheless. "Very well, *Captain*." He offered a clumsy bow, his injuries making it difficult to accomplish the gesture smoothly. "I'm glad you're all right," he said before he turned to leave.

"I'm glad you are, too," Kyle offered.

Nico waved her off and was gone, the door shutting softly behind him.

"He also came to tell us what's been going on while we've been asleep," Teague explained, padding to their side of the bed. They climbed under the covers beside Kyle, snuggling in and making themself comfortable. "Apparently, Valeria and those she now leads have been nothing but polite and accommodating since they lost their overbearing elder. The fact that you saved them from that horrendous maelstrom seems to have lessened their loyalty to Vána's previous cause."

"Considering that they're on my ship, which they commandeered, then depended on me to get them to safety, it's the least they could do," Kyle offered wryly. She laid back down, gingerly favoring her injuries. Once she was comfortable, she extended her good arm and adjusted Teague's position so that they rested their head on Kyle's shoulder, curled up at her side.

"I thought so as well."

Kyle took the time to brush Teague's hair away from their face, tucking it gently behind their ear. She studied them while she did this, looking for any sign of distress or pain. Their face was calm, but Kyle still worried. Teague didn't always show or immediately share their stress. "Are you all right?" she finally asked.

Teague smiled and gave a slight nod. "I believe so. Perhaps a bit restless after all of the excitement. I'm also *very* happy to see skies without storms in them." They paused, then added. "Happy to see skies at all. Working in the kitchen and sleeping in carpentry storage has made me never want to see the orlop deck again."

"I could understand that."

"I'm just not sure of what to do with this restless energy."

Kyle grinned wolfishly. "I could make a suggestion or two."

Teague gasped and playfully swatted at Kyle's shoulder. "No. There will be plenty of time for that after you've done some healing, Captain."

Kyle let out an exaggerated groan as a pang of pain radiated from her burned arm. "*Fine*. Be that way." She pulled Teague closer, relishing the warmth and comfort that emanated from them. Kyle was content to stay like that for a few minutes, silent, basking in the glow of the morning. She knew it had to end sometime but couldn't help wanting it to last forever.

"How long do we have before we have to start being responsible?" Kyle asked, pouting.

"You will have all the time you need, Kyle. I will make sure of it, whether you like it or not." Teague sat up a bit to meet Kyle's gaze. "You have been injured and need to recover. As for me." They stopped to think, then continued. "Maybe an hour or two?"

They both fell quiet for a bit and Kyle let her mind drift. Without fail, her thoughts slipped back to the day before.

Vána Raudnost was dead. Her mother's mother. Her *grandmother*. Just thinking the word was painful. The realization hit her hard. A flash of grief welled up inside Kyle, taking her by surprise. Despite recent events, Kyle found herself reaching back further in her recollection. She thought back to when she was young, when Vána had been more of a grandmother. The memories were few, but there were more than a handful of a much younger Kyle being offered Adalarian candy and beautifully embroidered skirts by Vána. What could have been if Meliandra hadn't died? Or if Vána had cared more about her grandchild?

A sob bubbled from Kyle's lips, surprising both Teague and herself.

"Hey," Teague offered, squirming a bit to position themself on the pillow next to Kyle. They brought their hands up to either side of Kyle's face, cradling it and wiping at her falling tears with their thumbs. "Where are your thoughts?" they asked.

Kyle sniffled and chuckled softly. "I'm not sure where this came from. I haven't truly thought of Vána as family in more than a decade. She never showed interest and I was just a kid whose Ma had just died. It felt like my grandmother abandoned me. As if I wasn't worth the effort." The more she spoke, the faster the tears fell.

Teague just offered a gentle smile and kissed Kyle's forehead. "Grief is a strange force. Perhaps part of you mourns what might or could have been. Or maybe it has been a very *long* couple of weeks."

Kyle laughed again. "You are not wrong." She took some deep breaths, letting herself be held and passing through the waves of emotion.

Once the tears dried and she was able to breathe without sniffling, she let out a soft sigh and pulled the blankets up to her chin, burrowing into their comfort and warmth. She was beginning to feel sleepy again, and since Teague had said they had some time, she wanted to take advantage of as much as she could. She felt herself beginning to drift off, feeling safe in her own bed with Teague by her side.

"Feeling better?" Teague asked.

Kyle nodded wordlessly and didn't open her eyes, too comfortable to strive to keep awake.

After a brief pause, she heard Teague ask, "So, we're still getting married?"

"I haven't asked yet," Kyle said, sleepily.

"Oh?" Teague sounded amused. "Are we going to attempt to do the night over, then?"

Kyle yawned. "Well, you said we needed to be elaborate, and I want to get it right. I wouldn't want you to refuse me because of a botched proposal." She smiled.

"Is *that* the only reason I'd refuse you?"

"Of course," Kyle said quickly, but a wisp of doubt slithered at the back of her mind. She opened her eyes, blinking tiredly as she gazed at Teague beside her on the pillow. "Right?"

"I doubt I would refuse you on something so trivial," Teague retorted, wrinkling their nose. "As long as you have no other relatives like your grandmother, I am sure that whenever you ask me, the answer will be yes."

"Don't worry, love," Kyle said on the back of yet another yawn. She let her eyes drift shut. "It's just Da now, his parents, and Nico. My grandparents are much more like Da anyway."

"That... isn't as reassuring as you think."

"I know. That's why I said it." Kyle giggled and pulled Teague closer.

Kyle knew there would be challenges moving forward. She still had her aunt to return to port, her brother and father to see back to health, and her crew to pick up from Saltskiff.

By the depths, she had a new proposal to plan.

All of it was a problem for another day.

Right then she was content to hold fast to her love and drift back to sleep as *The Stargazer* sailed on.

Author's Note

You've made it! You've reached the end of Kyle's adventure. But never fear...Kyle, Teague, Nico, and a few others *will return!*

If you've been following me or my writing for a while, you may have a distinct feeling of déjà vu with this title. You would be right, by the way. "The Elysium Proposal" first appeared among a collection of other amazing stories published by Skullgate Media in August of 2021. This collection, *In The Wake of the Kraken: Pirates of the Multiverse*, was a gathering of short stories set in a world that all of the other authors and I *created* and then set our stories in. We all agreed that the world (or worlds) would be openly available for any of the authors to use in their own separate writings moving forward, so a few of the places you see in this story were born there (such as The Saltskiff Bazaar and the Elysium Cove). It was one of the most fun collaborative projects I've ever participated in. I am so proud of the work that we did for that book. If you ever want to read it, you can find it, and many other amazing independent authors' works here at SkullGateMedia.com.

Also, only certain readers may have caught this, but a character appeared from another book! I love the idea that my books could be alternate timelines or parallel universes for my friends' writing, so I'll include their characters from time to time. In this instance, Amara Lynn allowed me the use of their main character (Lamark) from their book, *Into the Deep*. If you're curious about Lamark's origins and want to read a sweet, steamy, and adventurous pirate novel, you can check it and more of their books out at their website, https://amarajlynn.com/.

As always, it takes a village to publish a book (or something like that) and although this village is a bit smaller this time around, I am still endlessly grateful to those who have helped me get this short story transformed into a novella and helped me get Kyle's story out to the world.

Michael Bross, my critique partner (and spouse), is first and foremost. I'm not sure where I would be without all of his "This needs more tension" and "Body language?" comments on my drafts. He is also a published poet in his own right, and if you are interested in some of his fantastic work, you can find his books at Finishing Line Press.

RJ Sorrento, my best friend and first among my beta readers, is always there to bring more depth and understanding to my work. Without their encouragement and enthusiasm about my writing, it would take much more to get anything done. So, thank you both from the depths of my heart. I appreciate you both and all that you do.

Finally, I want to say a huge thank you to my readers. You all are with me through thick and thin, and you understand that while I may write across different genres, you're still getting the found family and depth of character we all know and love. Thank you for being here and taking this journey with me.

ABOUT THE AUTHOR

A.E. Bross is a nonbinary, genderfluid indie author interested in fantasy in all of its forms, as well as romance, science fiction, and horror. When not getting lost in their writing, they are an academic librarian, passionate about open education resources and information literacy. They reside in the mountains beyond the Greater New York area with their spouse, kiddo, and two feline grandchildren.

Other Books by A.E. Bross

The Sands of Theia Fantasy Series
The Roots that Clutch
Under Stone and Shadow
No Light from the Fires

Modern Mages
Where We Converge